THE GUNSMITH

431

The Science of Death

THE GUNSMITH

431

The Science of Death

J.R. Roberts

SPEAKING VOLUMES, LLC
NAPLES, FLORIDA
2017

The Science of Death

ISBN 978-1-62815-750-5

Chapter One

Clint Adams wasn't the sort of man to drink himself into a stupor. He'd seen too many men get themselves killed by pouring an entire bottle of whiskey down their throat, shooting their mouth off and then assuming they could shoot their pistols just as well. With very few exceptions, that just wasn't the case. For every gunman who'd bitten off more than he could chew in a fight thanks to the liquor he'd drank, there were those who wound up sleeping in a gutter face down in horse piss.

Every now and then, however, drunkenness was damn near unavoidable. Some nights were just too rowdy to experience while sober. Some saloons were too wild to traverse without becoming another member of its wild life. And some women were too big of a handful to tame without some liquid courage.

Isabelle Karnov was a woman who not only encouraged drunkenness but enforced it, like a judge quoting the letter of the law. She was a wild woman with thin streaks of silver shot through her raven-black hair. Small wrinkles around her eyes gave away the fact that she was no spring chicken, which suited her just fine. She spoke loudly and if she didn't like someone, man or woman, she would do everything from tease them to take a swing at them. If she liked someone, on the other hand, she made that someone feel like they'd just become the luckiest man or woman on the face of the earth.

Clint met her in a filthy saloon about twenty miles south of Houston, Texas. He might have known the name of the town that saloon was in when he'd first arrived, but that bit of knowledge along with two entire days slipped away from Clint's mind quicker than greased ball bearings through a clumsy fist. He'd started off playing poker and as soon as Clint swept away most of the money from that table, Isabelle had come along to help him spend it.

She smelled like jasmine, tobacco smoke and beer. Her hands were all over Clint's body from the moment she introduced herself. At first, he'd thought she was trying to pick his pocket. Then, when she actually did reach into his pocket, she wasn't interested in the money he'd stashed in there.

"You're quite the man," she growled while cupping his penis through his clothes.

"My name's Clint. What do you—"

Anything else he'd wanted to say was lost when she locked her mouth onto his and slid her tongue between his lips. While her actions were aggressive, they were anything but clumsy. Instead, she just seemed like a woman who knew what she wanted and didn't like to wait.

"I want to ride you all fucking night," she'd said in a voice that reeked of alcohol but without a single slur.

"All right, then," Clint said. "I know just the place."

Clint's rented room was in a sleepy hotel that was all but abandoned. At least, he didn't get a chance to check for other guests because Isabelle was climbing all over him before he could get his key in the door.

"Give me a second," Clint protested while fumbling for his key. But Isabelle had already pulled off most of the buttons on the front of his shirt and yanked it open.

"Let me just . . ." Clint said while fidgeting with the lock.

But Isabelle merely chuckled and dropped to her knees so she could pull open Clint's pants. He glanced around anxiously, concerned not as much for his modesty as he was in getting tossed out of the hotel by its owner. When Isabelle reached between his legs and freed his cock so she could wrap her lips around it, he stopped being so concerned.

Clint leaned back against his door and slid his fingers through Isabelle's hair as her head started bobbing back and forth. She worked her mouth on him expertly, sucking at just the right time and tightening her lips around him to make him feel every last stroke right down to his toes. Just as his eyes were about to roll back in their sockets, she stopped and looked around.

"Someone's coming," she said in a hurried whisper.

"You got that right."

"No, I mean someone . . . let's just get inside that room!"

Clint opened the door and was shoved inside by Isabelle. A few seconds later, heavy footsteps thumped down the hallway. Isabelle stood looking through the narrow crack left by the mostly closed door. Once the steps passed by, Clint opened the door a little more so he could get a look as well.

"Who was that?" he asked when he caught a glimpse of a rotund older man waddling around the corner and disappearing from sight.

"My uncle. He's very protective."

"And he thinks you're a school teacher or something?" Clint chuckled.

"No! He just doesn't like seeing me doing . . . what I do best."

"And what's that, exactly?" Clint asked.

Isabelle turned to face Clint directly, placing a hand flat on his chest so she could push him away from the door. With her other hand, she shut the door and locked it. She had a good amount of strength behind her when she shoved Clint toward the narrow bed that took up most of the space inside the room. With just a few tugs on some ribbons and the loosening of a few hooks, she was able to wriggle out of her dress and let it fall into a heap around her feet. All she wore after that was a garter belt holding up a pair of tattered stockings and boots that laced up to the slope of her muscled calves.

"You think you can handle what I do best?" she purred.

"I'm not sure," Clint said as he hurried to get out of his clothes, "but I aim to find out."

Chapter Two

Isabelle's body was perfectly made for one thing and it was the thing she claimed to do the best. Those words turned out to be anything but empty. Once Clint hit the bed, she climbed on top of him, straddled his hips and reached down to stroke his pole. He became erect in a matter of seconds and slid in between her wet pussy lips with ease.

"That's the way," she said, as if she was smiling down at an inexperienced boy. "Just lay back and let me do the work."

She placed her hands flat on Clint's chest and rocked back and forth. For a short while, Clint let her take charge. He used that time not only to watch her pendulous breasts sway near his face, but to catch his breath after being wrangled all the way to that spot like an unruly horse.

Soon, his hands found Isabelle's wide hips and grabbed on with a firm grip.

"Well now," Isabelle said as she looked down at Clint and dug her nails into his chest. "Feeling wild, yourself?"

He answered that by pumping up into her with strong, powerful strokes. After a few solid thrusts, he pushed inside of her and stayed there so she could feel his erection becoming harder.

Isabelle's eyes widened and she gazed at Clint with new-found respect. "You're not just another handsome cowboy, after all! Good."

She rocked back and forth on top of Clint as if she was in a rodeo. When he reached up to cup her breasts with both hands, Isabelle arched her back, tossed her hair and clamped her hands over his to keep them in place. She grunted and groaned every time he buried his cock inside of her, snarling hungrily for more.

Clint sat up and held her buttocks in both hands. Not wanting to be thrown off of him, Isabelle locked her hands behind his neck and wrapped her legs around him. She wasn't a light woman, but Clint didn't need to carry her far. Once he'd gotten out from under her, he set her down on the bed and opened her legs.

"Oh yes," she said excitedly. Isabelle reached down to spread herself open so Clint could pump into her easily. "God damn! Just like that!"

Clint stood next to the bed with her laying on its edge. He gripped one of Isabelle's ankles in each hand, spreading her legs open wide as he pounded between her thighs. The harder he fucked her, the more she hollered for more.

"Come on," she urged. "Come . . . on . . ."

Isabelle's entire body stiffened and she grabbed the mattress on either side of her. Her eyelids fluttered and her pussy cinched in tight around him. When she opened her eyes again, she looked even more ravenous than before.

"Oh, you've done it now," she growled. "Time for me to show you some more."

Clint was ready for any lesson she had to offer. First, Isabelle climbed off the bed and pushed Clint back onto it. Having traded places, she stood beside the bed and Clint lay on it with his legs hanging over its side. Isabelle climbed on top of him once more, only this time she turned around to sit on his face and lower her head between his legs.

She immediately began sucking his cock, teasing him until he started licking her. Clint tasted her only a few times before he could barely see straight. Either her new angle of attack was making a difference or she truly was the best at what she did because every nerve ending in his body started to hum. Clint grabbed onto her backside, burying his tongue between Isabelle's legs for a few more seconds until she took him over the edge.

When he climaxed, Clint felt the entire room tilt on its side. Of course, that could have been caused more by all the liquor in his system. Whatever the reason, it didn't last nearly long enough. Sensing when the sensations were starting to ebb in his body, Isabelle used her tongue on him in just the right way to extend Clint's pleasure for a little while longer.

After a while, he had to nudge her away. "Let me catch my breath," he said. "You're gonna kill me."

Isabelle crawled off of him, dabbing at the corner of her mouth with one finger. "You wouldn't be the first," she said.

Clint had no trouble believing that whatsoever.

Chapter Three

Clint staggered out of his room some time later. Could have been a few hours. Could have been a few days. With Isabelle only leaving the room to get more liquor for them both, it was difficult for Clint to be sure. All he did know was that she was gone and he was hungry enough to eat an entire grizzly bear and then ask for seconds.

"Finally up and at 'em, huh?" asked the elderly man behind the front desk. He wore bent spectacles and a black vest over a stained white shirt. A ledger sat in front of him and a fountain pen was clutched in his hand. He looked more than willing to be distracted from his bookkeeping, however.

"What time is it?" Clint asked.

"Little after ten."

"Mind telling me what day?"

"Saturday," the clerk said with a chuckle. "Did you think you slept through until Sunday?"

Fortunately, Clint's eventful night had only been seven hours ago. Unfortunately, his head felt as though it had been cracked open with a shovel. "Are you still serving breakfast?" he asked.

"Not since about eighteen months ago," the clerk replied. "The Canary serves some mighty good biscuits, though."

Clint let out a groan when he heard the name of the saloon where he'd met Isabelle. The thought of even smelling liquor at this point made his stomach churn. Plus, he was royally pissed at himself. Even though he had only been playing penny ante poker with some locals, he usually never drank when he played cards. Last night he had been stupid, and he was lucky to still be alive.

"Anywhere else?" he asked.

"Not this late in the day. Lunch'll be served in an hour or so down at Miss Penny's."

Clint didn't know where Miss Penny's was and he wasn't about to ask. He gave a quick thanks to the clerk, headed out the door and went to the one place where he knew he could get some good food. If memory served him correctly, The Canary had a decent cook.

When he arrived, the place was quieter than the night before. Clint found a table against a wall and sat down. In less than a minute, a woman in her late twenties approached him with a pot of coffee in one hand and a mug in the other.

"You must be feeling rotten," she said.

Clint rubbed his eyes. "Yeah. There's plenty of reasons I normally stay away from whiskey and last night was a good one."

"Why change your habits?"

"I got talked into it by a very persuasive woman."

"That's right," she chuckled. "Isabelle had her sights set on you. I'm surprised you can walk straight."

"Me, too." Clint sipped his coffee and let out a slow sigh. "This tastes strange but . . ."

Smirking at the perplexed expression on Clint's face, the woman said, "But it makes you feel better, doesn't it?"

"It does."

"There's an egg in there along with some of the shell."

Clint winced and swirled the coffee around in his mug. "Good lord."

"Just sip it slow," she said. "The shell stays at the bottom mostly. It'll settle your stomach. How about something to eat?"

"I'm starving."

Before he could tell her what he wanted, the server said, "I'll bring you some biscuits and honey and a few pieces of bacon. Anything more and you'll just puke it back up again."

"No, I won't."

But she wasn't having any of it. "I've cleaned up enough messes from men in your condition to know what's best for them. You'll eat what I bring you or you'll be the one doing the cleaning."

Not wanting to argue any further, Clint nodded and waved impatiently at her. The waitress must have been used to dealing with aggravated drunks because she chuckled lightly to herself and went to the kitchen where she hollered her order at the cook loud enough for everyone in the vicinity to hear it. Clint's head was pounding so hard that he barely even noticed the arrival of two more customers.

"Hey!" one of the new arrivals shouted. "What the hell are you doin' here?"

Clint rubbed his temples and took another drink.

A few seconds later, a heavy hand dropped onto his shoulder, causing him to spill some of his coffee.

"I asked you a question, asshole," the man said.

"And I heard you," Clint snarled.

"Then what've you got to say for yourself?"

Clint looked up, squinted and looked back down again. "Do I know you?"

"You should. You took what was mine last night."

Looking up again put a pained scowl on Clint's face, mostly because moving his head in that direction felt like he was scraping his brain against a wall of broken glass. The harder he tried to focus, the more his eyes were squeezed within an invisible vice.

The man standing near him was dressed in filthy clothes, had unruly stubble sprouting from his chin and dirt caked onto one cheek. He seemed incapable of drawing a breath with his mouth closed, displaying several uneven gaps between his yellowed teeth.

Behind him stood a taller man who had the look of someone who prided himself on being feared. He had a bulky upper body wrapped in a cotton undershirt with the sleeves ripped off to show his muscular forearms. A protruding gut and droopy eye kept him from being mistaken for a prizefighter, even though he had the feral snarl down pat.

After a few more seconds, Clint turned back around to his table. "You don't look familiar, but then again I was pretty drunk last night." And stupid, he added to himself. If he'd encountered these two while drunk, he truly was lucky to still be alive. What the hell had he been thinking?

"Damn right you were," said the dirty man. "Otherwise you would've listened when I told you to mind your own damn business."

"Wait a second," Clint said. "Maybe I do remember. You were at the card table, right?"

"That's right."

"And I won your watch with a pair of queens."

"No," the dirty man grunted. "You pulled the lady away that was sittin' on my lap!"

"Oh, that's right. You were calling her some foul names and slapping her on the face."

"I called her what she was and I barely tapped her god-damn face!"

Clint finished his coffee, making certain he didn't accidentally get any of the eggshells. "There's no reason for a man to slap a woman."

"Which is exactly what I told you last night. Ain't none of your goddamn business." The dirty man punctuated his statement by slapping the hat off of Clint's head.

Letting out a beleaguered sigh, Clint slowly pushed back from the table and got to his feet. He turned around to find both men standing shoulder to shoulder with each other to form a wall of stinking, ugly flesh between his table and the door. Fortunately, Clint had no intention of trying to escape.

"I understand I was drunk last night," Clint said. "And I understand I embarrassed you in front of your friend. Sorry about that."

"We don't give two shits about you bein' sorry," said the larger of the two men.

Those words were enough to cause the restaurant's only other customer to creep away from his table and head for the door.

"Fine," Clint said. "So just pick up my hat, hand it to me and be on your way."

"Pick it up your own goddamn self," the ugly man said.

"If you're worried about impressing that lady, then don't trouble yourself. You wouldn't have been able to handle her."

The ugly man's face twisted into an even less appealing mask as he charged at Clint like a bull.

Chapter Four

It was a fairly quiet morning in the little town. No cattle drives were coming through. No festivals were tearing through the streets and there was no unrest among the native tribes in the area. It was quiet by anyone's standards . . . right until the moment when two men exploded through the front window of the restaurant on First Street.

The ugly man's back was what shattered the glass pane and the rest of him came through like a boulder. Clint's arms were wrapped around his midsection, keeping his body in close so he could steer the angry man while shoving him at the same time. Having tripped on something inside the restaurant, the ugly man lost his footing and was nowhere close to regaining it as he was sent outside.

Following close behind, the ugly man's bulky companion stepped through the decimated window. He circled around the other two, looking for a good spot to insert himself into the fray.

Both men who'd destroyed the restaurant's front window landed on their sides. Still locked in a tight grapple, they rolled a few times on the ground before coming to a stop in the middle of the street. The ugly man wound up on top of Clint and he took full advantage by pummeling Clint's ribs with an assault of chopping punches.

After weathering the initial storm, Clint drove his fist into the ugly man's kidney which robbed him of his next breath.

Now that the punches had stopped, Clint rolled away from him and scrambled to his feet.

The first thing Clint saw once he was upright was the carriage rolling toward him. It wouldn't run him over because it was already being drawn to a halt. The same thing couldn't be said, however, for the big fellow that rushed at Clint while gaining steam with every step. Clint tried to brace himself but could barely tense his muscles before he was knocked off his feet.

With the first man, Clint had been able to absorb the initial blow that had started the fight before driving the dirty man through the window. This time, Clint could only hope he'd be able to get up again. The impact of the large man running into him was like what he might feel after getting run down by the nearby cart. Before he could recover from that, Clint was doubled over by a thumping punch to the gut.

"Git him, Clyde!" the ugly man shouted. "Hold him steady for me!"

Clyde lunged forward to grab Clint with both hands. Clint brought his arms up and out to either side to knock away the two muscled arms that meant to entrap him. Then, Clint followed up with a quick series of punches delivered to the bigger man's stomach and ribs.

One after the other, Clint's fists pounded into Clyde's body. His knuckles didn't do much damage, even as they continued to pepper the big man with a string of punches. After a short, grunting laugh, Clyde grabbed Clint by the collar and swatted him in the side of his head.

Where Clint had been feeling a nasty headache before, that last punch made him wish his head would just be knocked off his shoulders altogether. His ears filled with a loud ringing sound and he nearly lost his balance. Once he felt the big man's meaty hands close around his neck, Clint knew he had to act fast before he lost consciousness or was choked to death right there in the street.

"Sorry 'bout this," Clint grunted before slamming his knee between the bigger man's legs.

Clyde's eyes grew wide and his grip loosened just enough for Clint to pull away. The big man wasn't down for the count, however, so Clint finished him off by clasping both hands together and attacking him as if he was swinging an axe handle. The powerful blow landed squarely on Clyde's chin, dropping him to the dirt.

That left two men standing in the street. Clint squinted as his head continued to throb and the ugly man stood poised only a few paces away. The other man's eyes darted back and forth to Clyde's bulky, squirming form. The big man didn't seem ready to get up anytime soon.

"You must really think you're somethin'," the ugly man sneered.

"Last night I was just drunk," Clint said. "And today I was just trying to eat some breakfast."

"You strutted in just to make me look like a damn fool!"

"Seems like you do a good enough job of that on your own," Clint replied.

The ugly man bared his teeth and tensed his right arm. Clint had been aware of the holster strapped around his waist from the moment he'd first laid eyes on him. The only thing keeping the ugly fellow alive this long was the fact that he hadn't yet reached for his shooting iron.

Without showing the first hint of fear, Clint walked slowly toward the other man. "What's your name?" he asked.

The ugly man recoiled slightly and took a step back. "Hunter," he said.

"Hunter, until now I didn't even know you were alive. Last night, I had eyes for the lady you were with and she wound up with me. That's all there is to it and, to be honest, I'm sure you still have just as much chance with that same lady today as you did yesterday."

Having retreated another two steps, Hunter held his ground. Clint did the same, standing directly in front of him.

"Considering the ache I got in my head," Clint said, having you shoot me right now might be a blessing. Even so, I doubt you'll get the chance. If you try it, you'll wind up dead and it'll be just for a bit of embarrassment. You want that, or would you like to consider it a draw after tossing me around and having your friend knock me to the ground a few times?"

There was still some anger in Hunter's eyes, but it was a far cry from the burning rage that had been there before. His thoughts took a wrong turn for a moment, causing his hand to reach toward his holstered pistol. Before he could get a solid grip on the gun's handle, Clint had already lifted his Colt halfway from its resting place at his side.

Hunter swallowed hard as Clint gave him a lingering, questioning stare.

Nothing else needed to be said. Hunter averted his eyes from Clint, turned around and walked away.

Clint stepped back into the restaurant so he could have a word with the owner.

Outside and down the street a short ways, a short man with a round belly leaned out from behind the post where he'd been standing when the two fighters had come bursting through the window. He watched as Clyde pulled himself up and staggered to catch up with Hunter. Then he adjusted the thick spectacles on his nose and nodded.

"Interesting," he mused. "How very interesting."

Chapter Five

"Sorry for the mess," said the owner of the restaurant as he swept up the last bits of broken glass. "Had a bit of a scuffle."

The portly bespectacled fellow smiled widely enough to cause the ends of his thin mustache to curve upward. "No need to explain. I saw most of what happened. Is everyone all right?"

"Just a few scrapes and bruises, is all. Might be better if you came back in a while."

The owner's plea was cut short when he saw the folded bit of money being handed to him by the portly man. The owner took the cash, tucked it away and motioned toward a few of the tables in back of his place. "Pick one of the tables there. I'll have someone come to take your order."

"I'll just have some hot tea and bread. Thanks."

"Be right out."

There was only one other person in the restaurant who didn't work there. One other man sat at a table in the back with his head down and a plate in front of him. He didn't look up and he didn't acknowledge the portly man's presence.

"You might want to pick a table on this side of the room," said the serving girl as she stepped out of the kitchen. "The gentleman at that table in the back has had a hard day."

"I know," the portly fellow replied. "I've seen a good portion of it." Smiling, he walked over to the table at the back and pulled up a chair.

"You heard the lady," Clint said in a rough voice. "Pick another table."

"But I came to see you, sir."

Clint's head had been angled downward to keep most of the light from his eyes. As he looked up slowly, the brim of his hat lifted to reveal a greater portion of his face. There were fresh scratches from broken glass, red blotches from where he'd been hit and dark circles under his eyes.

"What the hell do you want?" Clint asked.

"My name is Carmine Bertolucci. Doctor Carmine Bertolucci, actually. Perhaps you've heard of me?"

"Can't say that I have."

"Well, that's not too surprising. I imagine you don't exactly travel in intellectual circles." The doctor's eyes suddenly widened. "Not to say that you're stupid! All I meant was—"

"Whatever you want to say, do it fast," Clint grunted as he shifted his attention back to his plate. "I'm in no mood for small talk."

"Great. Good. Do you mind if I sit down?"

"Suppose not."

"That coffee smells good, but I imagine it could use some extra flavor," Bertolucci said.

Eyeing the doctor suspiciously, Clint said, "Maybe it's best if you leave, after all."

The doctor's round face brightened with a smile as he reached into one of the interior pockets of his suit coat. He produced a small vial and presented it to Clint like a magician who'd created a dove from thin air. "This will help your headache."

Clint furrowed his brow.

"Look, I'll try some myself," Bertolucci said. He then took a small sip from the vial and grinned. "Just a little?"

Grudgingly, Clint shoved his cup toward the strange man. Bertolucci poured a small splash of the liquid into the cup and then put the vial back in his pocket.

"Can't be worse than what's already in there," Clint grumbled. He took a small sip at first. When he felt a cool wave roll through his mouth, he took a larger one. "What is this?" he asked.

"Simple formula, really. I made it to counteract the effects of alcohol in the system."

"And you just happened to have it on you?"

"This is something of a wild little town," Bertolucci explained. "I planned on imbibing a little while I was here and brought it to soothe me afterwards. I couldn't help but overhear you earlier when you were complaining of a headache."

It took some bit of thinking, but Clint eventually snapped his fingers. "You were sitting right over there when I first got here. Left before I sat down, is that right?"

"Yes, quite correct. Your behavior and the way you carried yourself was all too familiar. The way you carried yourself outside, while impressive, also showed some small bit of impairment."

"Worked out fine enough," Clint said with a shrug. He caught the eye of the serving girl and held up his cup. She nodded and went to get him some more coffee. "So, why are you here, Mister Bertolucci? You know the men who tossed me out that window?"

"Not very well, but I have seen them once or twice. This isn't my first visit here."

"You a lawman?"

"I already told you, I'm a doctor."

"Some lawmen have other jobs. How about you just say your piece? You obviously have something on your mind or you wouldn't have sat down."

"I have a proposition to make, sir."

"Not interested," Clint said.

"How can you say that?"

"Because you only talked to me after you saw me win a fight. That means you probably want to make some kind of offer that involves more fighting. Also, you're acting squirrelly, so I'm not interested."

"I'm just a bit nervous," Bertolucci said. "My proposition concerns some very peculiar circumstances that could very well shape the world as we know it."

"All right," Clint replied. "Now I'm a little interested."

Chapter Six

After the few sips he'd taken of the doctored coffee, Clint's head was already much clearer. There was also a minty coolness that wafted inside of him like a fresh breeze blown in from icy waters. The ache in his head was still there, but just barely.

Even with the headache, Clint knew the doctor wasn't a threat. There was a sense that a man developed which was honed every time someone tried to lie to him, stab him in the back or take a shot at him. It was a basic survival instinct that any animal needed to have if it wanted to live in a dangerous world. After all of the years he'd spent trading shots with some of the worst this dangerous world had to offer, Clint's instincts were sharper than most.

Even so, Clint wasn't about to buy whatever the doctor was selling. There were a few small tables in a back room that were mostly used by the workers at the restaurant to eat their meals without bothering paying customers. When Doctor Bertolucci asked for a bit of privacy, the serving girl mentioned the rooms to him. Since sitting there meant putting Clint out of sight in the event that anyone else came around looking for someone to throw through another window, the owner was more than happy to let them move their conversation back there.

Now that his senses were sharper, Clint could watch the doctor as he made his way to the back room. The first thing he noticed was that Bertolucci wasn't armed. At least, he wasn't wearing any weapon that he could get to in a hurry. Second, Bertolucci was nervous. It wasn't a suspicious kind of nervousness, but more of a general fidgeting manner about him which made him seem even less of a threat. It also leant some credence to the first thing Bertolucci said once he sat down at the small table in the dimly lit room.

"I generally don't condone violence," he admitted. "It makes me somewhat . . . queasy."

"Then why approach someone who just got his hands bloody in a street fight?" Clint asked.

"Because sometimes violence approaches even those who don't seek it out."

"Someone's after you?"

"Yes."

The serving girl stepped into the back room to deliver Clint's coffee. As she set it down, he said, "Did anyone ever tell you that you use a whole lot of words to say very little?"

"Yes," Bertolucci replied. "They have."

The server giggled at that and left the two men alone.

Once she was gone, Bertolucci said, "I'm working on something that has great potential uses and the possibility to benefit people on a potentially global scale."

"So it's important."

"Yes. Very."

"I think I've got it now," Clint said. "You just need to cut what you mean to say in half and that should do it. You'll save a lot of breath and time that way."

Glaring at Clint the way a teacher scowls at a smart-mouthed pupil, Bertolucci said, "I see you're feeling better."

"Yes, I am."

"Good. Now perhaps you can take this seriously?"

Clint leaned back in his chair while lacing his fingers across his stomach. Reclining as though he was enjoying a cool sway on someone's front porch swing, he said, "I don't know enough about what you're doing to take it seriously. All I know is whatever it is, you think it's important. Isn't that what you'd expect anyone to say when they're working on anything?"

Bertolucci took a breath and looked as if he was about to speak. Before he got a word out, he sighed, looked around and glanced back toward the main part of the restaurant. Even though there were only two other people out there who were more concerned with cleaning up the mess, Bertolucci dropped his voice to a whisper. "I'd rather not discuss it here."

"Then I'd rather not waste any more time with this," Clint said, mocking the doctor's whisper.

Both men sat back in their chairs, staring across the table at each other. Finally, Bertolucci said, "It involves powering steam engines, for a start."

"Last time I heard, those were powered by steam. Isn't that fairly easy to come by?"

"It's also a tedious and potentially expensive process. If you're talking about powering larger factories or more cumbersome locomotives, it could be nearly impossible."

"Making better trains? That could be a pretty valuable idea if you can get it to work."

"Not just making better trains, although that part of it will come," Bertolucci said, his excitement growing with every word. "I'm talking about making the trains we have now even better."

"All right. How?"

"By making them travel faster and more efficiently. There won't be the need for constant shoveling of coal and they'll be able to go for longer durations without having to stop for repairs and such."

"And how would you do that?"

"By changing the way we think about steam power," Bertolucci replied. "By inventing not only a new engine, but a new method by which that engine is powered."

Clint was intrigued by the idea, but wasn't having much success in wrapping his head around it. Although he could tell Bertolucci was more than ready to spell it out for him, Clint could feel his headache returning when he thought of all the potential scientific double-talk he'd have to endure along the way.

"I'm not an expert in any of this," Clint said. "All I know about trains is how to buy a ticket. What could you want from me?"

"I don't need you to help in the process of research and assembly. I've already got that covered. My problem is that a few men from various railroad interests have already caught wind of what I'm doing and want to either put a stop to it or take it for themselves. What I need is someone to handle that aspect of this venture so my assistant and I are free to continue our work unimpeded."

"So you need a guard dog."

"No, I need much more than that. I need someone I can trust as well as someone who can handle themselves."

"What makes you think you can trust me?" Clint asked. "As far as you know, I'm just someone who got drunk one night and got into a fight afterwards."

"I'm an impeccable judge of character," Bertolucci announced. "And I'm also willing to pay enough to make it worth your while."

Clint rubbed his chin and thought about that for a few seconds. "Care to tell me some more about this invention of yours?"

"I prefer to think of it more as an innovation."

"Fine," Clint sighed. "Care to tell me some more about this innovation of yours?"

"Unfortunately . . . no."

"Why not?"

"Because I can't reveal too much to someone without knowing them better. I need you for a simple job and knowing all of my discoveries isn't part of that job."

"Simple?" Clint scoffed. "Sounds to me like you're catching the attention of some men with large interests and pockets deep enough to protect them. There's been plenty of blood spilled where the railroad is concerned and that's just regarding simple things like land rights and workers' wages. If what you're talking about is even half true, there'll be a lot more reason for those railroad men to come after you."

"Indeed. Your job will be simple. Keep those potential threats away from me, my assistant and my work while avoiding any bodily harm yourself. That's it. Simple. I never said it would be easy, though. That's another word entirely."

Rather than bicker about words with someone who loved using them so much, Clint let it rest.

Chapter Seven

Clint Adams never thought he was taking jobs. For one thing, he really didn't need to. He had enough investments around the country—saloons, ranches, mines, casinos, in one case a riverboat—that he didn't need the money. So when he agreed to do something for somebody, it was usually to help a friend, or it was something he was just interested in.

As far as the job Doctor Bertolucci was offering, Clint wasn't quite sure about it just yet. Because the doctor seemed honest enough at first glance, Clint decided to give him a chance. Besides, there was nothing else on his plate, and getting drunk the night before because he was bored was still bothering him. So he decided to help the doctor. When the man heard that, he was overjoyed, to say the least.

"You won't regret this, Mister Adams! You'll see. You'll be doing a great service not only to the railroad business in general, but the regular traveler who wishes to see this great and vast land of ours."

"I said I'd sign on to the job for now," Clint said. "For now, not the entire ride."

"Of course, of course. You're free to go at any time."

"That goes without saying," Clint told him. "What I meant was that I'm warning you I might decide to walk out on this job and I won't hear about any talk of contracts or anything like that. I want to be paid by the day and that's got nothing at all to do with promises of working another day in the future.

The pay is for that day's work. No more." He didn't want to undervalue himself by doing the job for free. The doctor had to feel like he was paying for a service.

"Naturally," Bertolucci said with a vigorous nod.

The two men were walking down the curving street that cut through the middle of town. By the look and feel of it, the street might have been straighter at one time but had been forced to bend and slope due to flooding or some other bit of bad luck. To confirm Clint's theory, they occasionally passed a stack of charred wood marking the spot where a building had once stood. Rather than rebuild after the building had burnt down, the folks in that town decided to simply work around it and leave it be. It seemed even the locals didn't expect their town to exist for more than another year or two.

"I trust the money I already gave you will suffice for today?" Bertolucci asked.

When he'd agreed to work for the doctor, Clint had asked for his first payment up front. Part of that was to make sure the doctor was serious. Not only had Bertolucci readily agreed to Clint's terms, but he'd paid him from a thick wad of bills that had been tucked into his interior jacket pocket.

"Yes," Clint said. "That's more than enough for today. In fact, I was thinking I'd let that cover the next couple of days."

"Really? That's mighty generous of you! I'd be more than willing to cover your expenses or even add a bonus if you do a good enough job," he said while reaching back into his pocket.

Before the doctor had even gotten to his money, several muddy faces from the immediate vicinity were turning to look at him. The doctor's clothes weren't exactly fancy, but they were clean and in good repair which put him several steps above any of the locals to be found in that town.

Clint reached out to hold the doctor's arm so it couldn't move another inch. "You're fine. Just keep what you've got to yourself. Don't be flashing your money on the street."

"You truly are starting your job right away. That's admirable, but you don't have to worry about these good folks. I've been to this place several times to buy supplies and have been met with nothing but kindness."

"You see that fellow there?" Clint asked while nodding at a scowling vagabond leaning against an awning post at the corner they were approaching. "He's been sizing you up from the moment we came down this street."

"Perhaps he just admires my new hat?"

"Damn, you really do need a guard dog," Clint sighed.

As if on cue, the muddy-faced stranger narrowed his eyes as if he was looking at a pair of freshly spotted targets through a rifle sight. Clint discouraged the stranger by glaring right back at him and easing his hand toward the Colt hanging at his side. Whether it was because of the unspoken promise that had been given to draw the pistol or simply the fire in Clint's eyes, the stranger decided against making another move and settled back against his post.

"See?" Bertolucci said merrily while waving at the stranger. "There's nothing to fear."

When Clint accepted the job, he thought he'd have to arrange to meet the doctor sometime later for the work to begin. As it turned out, Bertolucci had only spotted Clint's street fight because he'd already been on his way to conduct the business that had brought him to town in the first place. The doctor barely wanted to wait long enough for Clint to finish his breakfast before moving right along.

Like an eager dog that had been freed from its leash, Bertolucci couldn't get out of the restaurant fast enough and had been leading the way down the street ever since. He'd also been talking about his scientific discoveries which was just a bunch of meaningless words to Clint.

It wasn't because Clint was too stupid to understand scientific talk. He'd had highbrow discussions with plenty of learned men over cigars and fine brandy. In this case, this particular man was all too leery about saying too much. The result of that was a whole lot of sentences lopped off in the middle followed by several stuttering attempts to rephrase before quickly steering to another matter entirely. After a while, Clint decided to just let the doctor talk and follow him to where he was going.

"Where is it we're going, anyway?" Clint asked.

"Oh, I need to see a man who is very well practiced in the fine art of metal working."

"You mean a blacksmith?"

"More than that, my good man. He's perfected a way to . . . well, let's just say he can infuse certain properties into iron that . . . how can I put it?"

"Don't worry about putting it anywhere," Clint said out of exasperation. "I think I see who you're talking about right now."

"Ah, yes," Bertolucci said as he looked in the direction Clint was pointing. "Let me have a word with him on my own. Just wait here."

"You sure about that?"

"Quite. We're both rather protective of our own little trade secrets."

Since the blacksmith worked in a small barn with doors that stood wide open, Clint was fine with letting the doctor go on ahead. It wasn't long, however, before a few men wearing guns on their hips started working their way closer to the front of that same barn.

"All right, then," Clint said to himself. "Time for me to earn some of my pay."

Chapter Eight

Clint had no intention of trying to overhear the discussion going on between Doctor Bertolucci and the blacksmith. That was a good thing because both men lowered their voices considerably the instant they noticed Clint and the other men drawing closer to the small barn. A few seconds later, the doors to the barn were swung closed.

There were three other men outside the barn with Clint. One of them circled around to the back of the barn while the other two approached Clint from either side. He didn't recognize any of them, apart from the gritty filth that seemed to be caked onto nearly everyone in the small Texas town.

"You have some horseshoes that need to be repaired?" Clint asked the larger of the two men.

The big man's face twisted into a scowl. "What the hell business is it of yours?"

"You might want to come back later," Clint offered. "Either that or find another blacksmith. I think this one will be busy for a while."

"Go fuck yourself."

"Excuse me?"

All Clint had to do was portray a small amount of hesitance in the way he spoke for it to be mistaken as weakness. Like any other predator, the big man sniffed it out and pounced right away.

"I said," the big man snarled as he strode up to stand directly in Clint's path, "go fu—"

Clint's hand snapped straight out to drive into the softest point of the big man's gut. Rather than simply punch the guy in the stomach. Clint pushed his hand forward as though he fully intended on reaching all the way through to the other side. "I'm sorry," he said. "Still didn't quite hear you."

The man's partner hurried over to him. Clint didn't need to turn and look behind him to know about that. He simply had to listen for the scraping of rushing boots against the dusty ground. When the scraping got close enough, Clint brought up his other arm and pulled it straight back until his elbow made contact with something solid. There was a muffled crunch followed by a gurgling moan.

Clint grabbed the first man by the shoulders and pulled him in close while bringing his knee up and out. Hitting the man in the same spot he'd just punched a few moments ago, Clint forced all of the air from the guy's lungs. After that, it barely took any effort at all to push him back.

Turning around, Clint got a look at the big man's partner. At the moment, the other man's most distinguishing feature was the bloody mess covering the middle of his face. The man clapped one hand against his face to stanch the flow of blood from his nose and made a puny effort to make a fist with his other hand.

On a whim, Clint grabbed the man's fist, twisted it the wrong way and then forced it back to slam into the guy's busted nose. "Oops," Clint said. "That must've hurt. You want me to step out of the way?"

After saying that, Clint pivoted around as if to clear a path for the groaning man with the bloody nose. One of Clint's feet swept in a short, strong line to catch the other man's ankle and kick his leg out from under him. Under normal circumstances, that wouldn't have been enough to knock the man down. Since this man was still reeling from the pain and dizziness that came along with a broken nose, he hit the ground harder than a sack of bricks.

Clint didn't waste another second before reaching down to pluck the guns from both men's holsters and race around to the rear of the building. Once there, he spotted the third man right away. That man spotted Clint as well, his eyes growing wide as saucers when he also saw the pistols gripped in Clint's hands. Ducking low as if those guns had already started firing at him, the man turned from Clint and the barn so he could run away as fast as his legs could carry him.

When Clint made his way around to the front of the barn again, both of the other two men were gone.

Chapter Nine

A few minutes later, the barn door creaked open and Bertolucci poked his head out. After taking a quick glance to either side, he asked, "Is everything all right out here?"

Clint stood nearby with his thumbs hooked over his gunbelt. "Sure," he replied somewhat sarcastically. "Why do you ask?"

"I just thought . . . never mind. Can you help me with something?"

"Sure."

The barn doors were opened and Bertolucci waved for Clint to come inside. Toward the back of the small barn, the blacksmith was lifting a flat box that was almost as wide as his torso. Even though the box was less than eight inches high, it was plain to see by the straining expression on the muscular smith's face that it was damn heavy.

"Think you could help with the rest of those?" Bertolucci asked, pointing to a short stack of similar flat boxes.

Clint pushed up his sleeves and headed into the blacksmith's barn. "Where are they going?"

"Onto that cart."

The cart was serviceable for the task of carrying a heavy load, but looked more suited to taking supplies from a store to a nearby home. More than likely, it was rarely used for anything other than making local deliveries. On top of that, the only animal in sight was a mule chewing idly on some hay.

"How far is it being hauled?" Clint asked.

"Just to the train station five miles from here."

"Is that mule the only thing pulling it?"

"Yes, but we should make it in time to catch my train," Bertolucci assured him.

"You'd better," the blacksmith grunted while hefting his box onto the cart. "Or you'll have to pay extra for the cart rental."

"No need for that," Bertolucci assured him. "We'll be on our way in no time at all. Isn't that right, Clint?"

"We'll be on our way even faster if you help carry some of these boxes."

"A fantastic idea!"

After that, the three of them loaded the cart without very many words passing between them. Actually, having the doctor's help didn't amount to much but it did lessen Clint and the blacksmith's chore by two or three boxes. After loading the cargo, Clint stepped back and swiped some sweat form his brow.

"How about a beer?" Clint said.

Bertolucci fretted at that, but couldn't get out much before the blacksmith slapped him on the shoulder and said, "Sounds like a fine idea to me. I bet the good doctor might even offer to pay for the first round. Ain't that so?"

"Uhh . . . well . . . we are on a schedule."

"Hardy ain't ready to go just yet," the blacksmith said while nodding toward the mule. "He still needs to eat and after he eats, he's gotta take a shit. That mule don't go nowhere until he's had his shit."

"That's understandable, I suppose," Bertolucci replied.

"It's settled, then! C'mon . . . what's yer name?" the blacksmith asked as he squinted in Clint's general direction.

"Clint Adams," he said.

"C'mon, Clint. Let's have some beer!"

As the two men left the barn, Bertolucci followed after them. "Just one or possibly two! We're on a schedule!"

Considering the blacksmith's silence throughout the loading of the cart, Clint was surprised at the amount of laughter erupting from the burly man after just a few long pulls of some fairly cheap beer. True to his word, Bertolucci paid for the first round. Once he saw just how cheap the beer was, he even sprung for the second round. After their mugs were emptied for the last time, he insisted on stepping out of the saloon.

"I've got work to do as well," the blacksmith said. "Guess I should start by hitching up that ol' mule to the cart."

"I'll give you a hand," Clint said.

"Splendid!" the doctor beamed. "I'll make a few last arrangements and we'll be on our way."

Clint and the blacksmith left the saloon. Once outside, Clint extended his hand and said, "I never caught your name."

"That's because I never gave it." The blacksmith's stern face lasted for all of three seconds before he let out a hearty belly laugh. "It's Kurt Ferguson."

As expected, Kurt's grip was beyond impressive. Clint did the best he could to return it, but knew he wasn't about to win a test of strength with the other man. Once they made it back to the smith's barn, Clint asked, "How long have you known Doctor Bertolucci?"

"Just under a year," Kurt replied as he opened the door and walked inside, "but this is only the third time I've ever seen him. Pays well, but doesn't know when to keep his mouth shut."

"Especially considering what he's working on," Clint said in an attempt to get some information out of the blacksmith. Even though Bertolucci was willing to part with some information, his answers were always guarded. Also, Clint figured he'd have an easier time understanding whatever the blacksmith had to say on the subject.

"Just some sort of charged iron," Kurt grunted.

"Charged? With what?"

Kurt looked over at Clint, the effects of his beers being washed away by some hard-edged suspicion. "Why do you want to know?"

Clint went to the mule's stall and reached for a bridle hanging from a hook on the wall. "Just curious."

"Aren't you working for Bertolucci?"

"Yeah, but he throws so many big words around it's hard to tell whether or not he's speaking English."

Kurt grinned. "Yeah, he does like to throw them words around."

"I just want to know if this is anything I should worry about, especially since I'll be the one lugging these boxes around when they're being unloaded." Clint didn't know that for certain, but he figured it was a safe bet. At least, it was something to remove some more of the suspicion from Kurt's mind.

The blacksmith shrugged while looking toward the doors of his barn. Nobody was right outside the building, so he said, "It's similar to a magnet, really."

"There's just a bunch of magnets in those boxes?"

"If you wanna look at it that way, yeah," Kurt replied. "My part in making that was in melting down the iron and casting it with another kind of metal."

Now that the bridle was on the mule, Clint started leading it toward the cart. Judging by the overpowering stench in that stall, Kurt had been right about the animal's willingness to move being connected to its bowels. "What kind of metal?" Clint asked.

"You'll have to ask the doc about that," Kurt replied. "He's the one that brought it. I'm just the one who did the casting."

"And the magnetizing," Clint said.

Kurt shrugged again, as if he was only willing to take partial ownership of that statement. Considering that the blacksmith still seemed on the verge of being suspicious of Clint all over again, the matter was dropped.

"Since you will be the one handling them boxes, I can tell you one thing," Kurt added. "Don't drop any of 'em."

"Why not?"

After thinking about it for a few seconds, Kurt opened his mouth to speak. Just then, the doctor's rambling voice could be heard from outside as Bertolucci approached the barn. "Just don't," Kurt said quickly.

And that was that.

The mule was hitched to the cart. Bertolucci shook hands with the blacksmith and their business was concluded.

Chapter Ten

Bertolucci was in such a hurry that he seemed surprised when Clint told him he needed to stop by a livery on the way out of town. "But we're on a schedule," the doctor said.

"You've mentioned that once or twice," Clint replied. "But I still need to pick up my horse."

"Your horse?"

"Yeah. I didn't walk into town, you know."

"Of course! Your horse. How silly of me! Why don't I just start heading out of town and you can catch up to me."

"I don't think that's a good idea."

"Why? Your horse isn't fast enough for the job?"

Clint laughed at the notion of Eclipse having any sort of problem outrunning a constipated mule pulling a cart loaded with boxes of iron.

"He's plenty fast," Clint finally said. "I just don't want you riding on your own."

He considered telling Bertolucci about the men who'd tried taking a run at the blacksmith's shop, but didn't want to waste any more time.

"You're paying me to keep an eye on you, so just let me do it properly."

"That makes sense."

The livery wasn't far away and when the stable boy came out to greet him, Bertolucci insisted on settling Clint's bill. Not long after that, Clint was sitting comfortably in his own saddle and riding alongside the cart.

"That is a fine horse," Bertolucci said. "Darley Arabian, am I right?"

"You are."

"I haven't seen one as nice as that since the last time I attended an impressive show put on by P.T. Barnum himself. Truly impressive."

"He gets the job done," Clint said proudly as he patted Eclipse on the side of the neck.

"My assistant will be very keen to get a look at him. Might even offer to buy him."

"Not for sale."

"I'm sure you'd get a hell of a price," Bertolucci added.

"Not for sale, doc. Not now. Not ever." He didn't bother telling the doctor that Eclipse was actually a gift from P.T. Barnum.

"Quite understandable."

Once the small town was behind them, Clint rode ahead a short distance to scout the trail. He came back, circled wide of the cart and took a quick look at the trail they'd left behind. When he returned, Clint fell into step with the cart once again.

"Stretching the horse's legs, eh?" Bertolucci mused.

"That and making certain nobody is following us."

"Following us?"

"Well, following you."

Now the doctor shifted in his seat, twisting to look over one shoulder and then the other before settling uneasily facing forward.

"What's the matter?" Clint asked. "Didn't you hire me to look out for you?"

"Yes, but hiring someone to stand guard is one thing. Coming to grips with the idea that I might actually be hunted is something else entirely."

"You seemed to be pretty comfortable with it back at that restaurant."

"I do better when I throw myself into a particular task," Bertolucci explained. "Keeps me distracted from the ugly truths that have been surrounding me of late."

"What can you tell me about the men who are after you?" When he saw the doctor's face turn pale, Clint added, "Just for the sake of conversation."

"I don't really know them personally. I mean . . . there's been more than one that's approached me."

"Did they bring hired guns along with them?"

"Not at first," Bertolucci explained, "but yes. Eventually."

When he'd started his questions, Clint's intention was to tell the doctor about the men who had tried to storm the blacksmith's place back in town. Perhaps he could see a reaction on Bertolucci's face that might let Clint know if there was something more that the doctor was hiding from him. Before long, though, there didn't seem to be a point.

One thing that Bertolucci wasn't hiding from him was the fact that there was something being hidden. In fact, he'd been quite clear about that very thing. What concerned Clint even more was that the doctor truly wasn't aware of just how much danger he might be in. Sometimes, it became easy for him to judge how treacherous and lethal other men could be. But for someone who didn't live their life by the gun, that sort of constant danger became easier to miss.

While he wasn't one to allow folks to stumble into mortal harm just because they were ignorant, Clint had something else to worry about. If even a portion of what Bertolucci was saying was true, it could be a very large worry indeed.

"So," Clint said before too long, "are you going to tell me some more about what's inside those heavy boxes?"

"I could, but it's all very dry talk. Mostly a lot of scientific terms that usually bore people after a few sentences."

"Mister Ferguson was telling me something about magnets."

"Really? When was that?"

"We spoke while we were loading the cart," Clint said. "He's a friendly sort once he gets to know you."

"Yes," Bertolucci said dryly. "And talkative, it seems."

"Was he supposed to keep it a secret?"

Bertolucci shrugged his shoulders and flicked his reins. "I guess not. He only knows one part of my experiment anyway."

"What's the other part?" Clint asked.

Bertolucci drew a quick breath, grinned and looked over at him. "You're trying to get information from me, Mister Adams."

"Yeah. That's usually why a man asks another man questions. He'd like some answers."

"We've only known each other a short time. For all I know, you could work for the men who are after my work."

"You know better than that."

"Do I?" Bertolucci scoffed.

Clint was dead serious when he replied, "Yes. You do. Otherwise, I wouldn't have come this far."

After a few more seconds of squirming in his seat, Bertolucci couldn't quite come up with his next words. He fidgeted for a short while before letting out a short, frustrated sigh.

"I know just how you feel," Clint said. "But you're a good judge of character."

"How do you know that?"

"Because you have a knack for letting good people work with you while aligning yourself against some real assholes. Kurt Ferguson was a good man and he's a talented smith. I know enough about the second part of that to be certain."

"If only you could give me your impressions of the others I've worked with," Bertolucci said.

"They must either be good folks or kept at a good distance. Otherwise, you'd be dead by now."

Keeping his eyes fixed on the trail ahead, Bertolucci said, "Look, Mister Adams-"

Clint put his hand out to stop the man.

"Might as well call me Clint."

Chapter Eleven

"Look, Clint, I'd like to illuminate you as to all of my work, but now is not the time."

"You're right about that."

Snapping his eyes over to Clint, the doctor asked, "What makes you say so?"

"Because there were some men who tried to take a run at you back at Ferguson's place."

Bertolucci smiled again. This time, it was warmer and more genuine than before. "I'm glad you told me about that."

"Wait. Did you already know about what happened while you were in there?"

"I didn't know all of the details, but I knew there was a scuffle of some kind. I may not be a fighter, but I am also not deaf."

"Did you know they'd be coming?"

"At that particular moment? No, but I knew they'd get to me before too long. Why do you think I hired you?"

"So why didn't you mention anything about it until now?"

Bertolucci blinked a few times, glancing over as if he was barely comprehending Clint's words.

"What's there to say? You did your job and I left you to it. When I do my job, I hope you'll show me the same consideration."

"All right, then. If you want to talk about my job, tell me what's in the boxes?"

"Not this again. If you'd like a more detailed explanation, why don't we save it for the train ride to Galveston? We'll have plenty of time for discussion."

"Where in Galveston?" Clint asked.

"Didn't we go over this already?"

"A bit, when I first agreed to the job. You told me you'd be more specific later."

"It's an island just off the Galveston coast," Bertolucci told him.

"What's it called?"

"Pebble Sands."

"Never heard of it," Clint said.

"Barley anyone has. That's why I didn't think it would matter if I told you or not. Actually, that's very similar to my reasoning of not spelling out an experimental procedure I'll be conducting to someone who doesn't have the knowledge necessary to fully grasp it."

Clint might have been angrier by the doctor's condescending tone if Bertolucci didn't have a good point. Since there was still a good portion of trail in front of them and Bertolucci was paying the bill, Clint played along and said, "Let's pretend I have something between my ears and might understand a word or two if you explained things to me."

Bertolucci let out a tired chuckle. "You'll have to excuse me. I've been trying to piece together this project for some time and the effort has only gotten harder as I get closer to actually producing something tangible. Every step of the way, there have been men who stand in my way either because they don't understand what I'm doing or wish to exploit it. All of that has made me a bit guarded."

"You're excused. Now, please continue."

"All right," the doctor replied in a somewhat excited tone. "The crates contain a particular kind of ore that has been treated much in the same way as a magnet."

"So your idea to improve the railroads has to do with magnets?" Clint asked.

"In a sense. At least, that's where my initial inspiration came from. The ore is a mixture of base elements . . .other metals that have been smelted into one. Are you very familiar with blacksmithing?"

Clint smiled at that. "A little."

"The process is fairly simple when dealing with typical materials like tin, iron and lead. Mixing in other, more exotic, materials is where things get tricky."

"How exotic are we talking?"

Bertolucci looked over at him tentatively. Although he seemed to want to explain, he fidgeted for a few seconds before saying, "Perhaps I can get into that later."

What the doctor meant, Clint knew, was that he might explain a bit more if he learned to trust Clint a little further. That seemed fair enough, so Clint didn't push the matter.

"For now," Bertolucci continued, "let's just say that the ore created by Mister Ferguson is something much more than just iron or tin."

"What else was melted into it?"

"It's not so much what was melted in, but what was done to each ingredient before it was added. You see, some of them

49

were treated with chemicals and some were refined to a nearly pure state. Others were melded with other elements such as silver or copper before being added into the whole. It's a very complicated process."

"Sounds like it," Clint said. "Is it explosive?"

"Explosive?" Bertolucci replied nervously.

"Yeah. Kurt told me to be careful with it. Made it sound like it might go off or something. Is that the case or not?"

"I wouldn't worry." As if on cue, the cart rolled over a large rock stuck into the ground. When the wheels bounced and shook the cart along with everything in it, the doctor winced and gripped his reins a little tighter.

"You sure about that?" Clint asked.

"It's not explosive," Bertolucci said. "But there may be some slight possibility of a reaction if the ore is beaten together with enough force."

"How much force?"

"I don't know exactly. I'd have to perform a proper experiment with a hammer and anvil and there's really no cause for that."

"Won't it be hit pretty hard if it's put to use on the railroad?" Clint asked.

Becoming more flustered by the second, Bertolucci said, "There's still a process to go through before it is put into use. That's why I'm taking it to my private laboratory instead of delivering it to the railroad buyers. Look, just be assured that I am aware of the dangers and will take measures to avoid them. The last thing I want is for my experiment to become dangerous. After all, that would defeat the purpose wouldn't it?"

"Depends on what your purpose is," Clint said.

Bertolucci laughed heartily and gave his reins a flick. "Well played, sir. Don't be worried about handling this ore. If it was so unstable, I wouldn't be transporting it myself and I certainly wouldn't ship it to my laboratory by train. After all, that wouldn't exactly put me in good graces with the railroads when it comes time to sell my innovation to them."

"True enough. But what about those men who might be coming after you?"

"What about them?" Bertolucci asked in a much more somber tone.

"Anything you can tell me might help. Especially since I'll be the one facing them down."

Shrugging, the doctor replied, "I've gotten some threats. A few nasty letters sent to my home in Dallas. A few gruff words passed to me and my assistant by some rough looking fellows."

"Were those men armed?"

"Nearly everyone is armed these days."

"Yes indeed. Some of those armed folks seem more likely to draw their pistols than others."

"I'm a man of science," Bertolucci said. "Violence doesn't make much sense to me. That's why I leave it to others."

"But that doesn't mean it won't come to find you."

"Which is why I've hired you, Clint. As for any other details regarding my antagonists, I'll have to think it over. When something useful comes to mind, I'll let you know."

From then on, Bertolucci's manner was lighter and even cheerful as he drove the wagon down the trail. Although Clint engaged in conversation whenever possible, he wasn't feeling quite so chipper.

Chapter Twelve

The train hadn't yet arrived at the station when Clint and Bertolucci got there. They had an hour or so to kill, during which Clint insisted they spend away from the station itself so they could watch for any suspicious happenings in that area. The only suspicious things he saw was a fat man waddling to the outhouse on three separate occasions and staying in there for prolonged amounts of time.

"You think he's dangerous?" Bertolucci whispered as they watched the fat man shuffle out of the shitter one more time.

"No," Clint replied. "But I think we should figure out what he ate so we can avoid it like the plague."

"Agreed."

A shrill whistle sounded in the distance, drawing the attention of both men to a length of track that stretched out to disappear to the south.

"Sounds like our train!" Bertolucci exclaimed.

"Could be. We'll wait here until it's time for them to load their cargo."

While the doctor was anxious to get moving, he wasn't about to go against Clint's decision. Both of them held their ground and stayed put as the train pulled to a stop at the platform and began unloading passengers and horses. Only a few large crates were taken off at that stop. After that, horses were led to the stable car and passengers were allowed to board.

"All right," Clint said. "Time to go."

Bertolucci was quick to snap his reins to get the cart moving forward again.

"Splendid! You really will like Pebble Sands. It's tranquil and the scenery can be quite breathtaking!"

The doctor prattled on without seeming to draw a breath and Clint let him go without saying a word in response. Clint's attention was focused on the trickle of passengers making their way to the platform. Some of them, such as a few small children and the mothers accompanying them, were obviously not a threat to anyone. The remainders were studied by Clint very carefully.

There was a tall man with a thinning beard and wispy strands of hair plastered down against his scalp. He wore a gun around his waist as well as a sneering expression that seemed to be permanently etched onto his face.

Then there was a slender fellow wearing small round spectacles. He was dressed in simple clothes; brown trousers and a dark vest over a wrinkled white shirt. Clint may not have paid too much attention to him except for the fact that the next two men to board the train were doing their best to catch up to the bespectacled passenger. No words were exchanged between them, but with one sharp backward glance, the man with the glasses got the others to back away from him and split off in different directions.

"Hold on for a moment," Clint said.

Bertolucci was just signaling a young man standing at the ramp where horses were loaded onto the train when he was stopped by Clint's sharp voice.

"What is it?" he asked.

"Just…wait."

Despite the growing impatience of the man trying to load the train, Bertolucci did as he was asked and kept the cart where it was.

Clint watched the passenger car for a few minutes without catching sight of the three men who'd caught his eye before. It wasn't much that had raised his suspicion, but it was more than he'd gotten from anyone else on the platform. Keeping his eyes and ears open for any hint of trouble, Clint nodded to Bertolucci and climbed down from his saddle.

"That wagon going with you?" the kid outside the livery car asked.

"No," Bertolucci replied, "but the crates are."

As soon as he saw the crates stacked in the back of the cart, the kid rolled his eyes and said, "I'll get some help."

"Never mind with that," Clint said. "I'll load them."

"You sure, mister?"

"Yep."

Not anxious to tackle the job if he didn't have to, the kid shrugged his shoulders and shifted his attention to another passenger with a horse that needed to be led onto the train.

The crates weren't too heavy, but Clint had allowed his mind to wander in several different directions during the ride to the station. He thought of dozens of different ways the crates could explode, catch fire or otherwise harm him if the simplest little thing went wrong during the process of loading them onto the train. For that reason, he took them from the cart one at a time even though he was strong enough to cut his work in half by doubling his load.

Fortunately, there weren't an abundance of crates to be loaded and Clint finished the job by the time the train whistle was sounding again.

"All aboard!" the conductor hollered.

"That horse going with you?" the kid asked while looking at Eclipse.

"You better believe it," Clint said as he wiped some sweat from his brow.

"He's a real beauty. Anything I should know?"

"Just make sure he gets a good view out a window and the freshest oats of the bunch."

When he saw the mild confusion drifting onto the kid's face, Clint flipped him a half dollar and added, "Just keep him comfortable, all right?"

"I can do that, mister!" the boy replied as he snatched the coin from the air.

The conductor stood outside the passenger car, calling out for any stragglers to hurry up and get on board. Steam was pushed through the pistons attached to the engine as smoke curled from the circular stack.

Clint looked around to find only a few other people on the platform with him. A round lady wearing a light blue dress and surrounded by a cluster of small children waved her handker-chief at one of the windows in the passenger car. When she got a half-hearted smile from a man inside the car, she waved harder and urged her children to do the same.

A lean man leaned in the doorway of the ticket office, watching the train while placing a cigarette in the corner of his mouth. He barely seemed to notice Clint's eyes on him as he struck a match against the door frame and touched the flickering little fire to his cigarette.

Bertolucci waited for Clint's nod before boarding the train himself. As the doctor climbed on, Clint watched the lean man smoking nearby. That fellow seemed more interested in blowing smoke rings than anything else, so Clint stepped off the platform and onto the train.

"Well that was nice and smooth," Bertolucci said as he picked a seat and lowered himself onto it.

Clint sat down as well, looked outside and immediately spotted the same folks on the platform. The women and her children were still waving. The lean man was still smoking his cigarette. Unfortunately, when Clint took a look at his fellow passengers, the man with the spectacles who'd boarded earlier was nowhere to be found.

Chapter Thirteen

Even though Clint would have always preferred to be in his saddle, reins in hand, while Eclipse tore down a stretch of open trail, it was nice to occasionally sit back and let someone else do the work. He knew some men who stubbornly refused to board a train because a steam engine was a mechanical abomination responsible for ripping apart the land they knew and loved.

Watching some of those iron horses make their way across the country while spitting smoke and ash into an otherwise clear sky, it was sometimes hard to argue with that point. Sitting inside one of them after a long ride, inside and dozing off every couple of minutes, Clint wasn't in the mood to argue much of anything.

The train had barely been going for two hours and Clint's frame of mind had already taken a turn for the better. He sat on a wooden bench with his hat angled slightly downward and his arms folded across his chest. As the train rumbled and clattered over its tracks, he was lulled into a sense of calm that he rarely got to enjoy.

"Hey," Bertolucci hissed as he swatted Clint's knee.

Clint shifted slightly, but didn't say anything before letting out a contented sigh.

"Hey!" the doctor said again, only slightly louder. "Wake up."

"I'm awake," Clint grunted.

"You were falling asleep."

"Is that not allowed on this job?"

"Did you see that man walk by?" Bertolucci asked.

"What man?"

"The one with the gun."

"You're one of the few men on this train that doesn't have a gun," Clint pointed out. "Stop being so squirrely."

"I'm not . . ." Bertolucci stopped short, looked over his shoulder and leaned in closer to Clint. "I'm not just nervous. Look and see for yourself. Quickly."

Clint blinked his eyes and sat up, realizing he was much groggier than he'd thought. After clearing his throat and forcing away the sleep that had been drawing in around him like a wet blanket, he looked in the direction Bertolucci had been trying to show him.

The man with the spectacles was there, standing at the front of the passenger car. He was talking to a couple of other men, whom Clint also recognized. They were some of the others who had caught his eye when the train was being loaded. Now that there was more of a reason to be wary of those other two, Clint studied them a little closer.

One looked to be the youngest of the three, which put him somewhere in his mid to late twenties. He had stringy, sandy brown hair that hung in a tangled mess down past his shoulders. His face was covered with scraggly, light brown whiskers that were unkempt as well. The unruly beard and drooping mustache, combined with his tussled mop of hair, gave him the appearance of a candle that had been lit for too long and was dripping wax all down its front.

The other one talking to the bespectacled man had darker skin and looked to be somewhere in his thirties. His face wasn't clean-shaven, but he had no real beard. With all the jagged scars marring his complexion, growing that much facial hair may have been impossible. Even before seeing the scabbards hanging from the man's belt, Clint had him pegged as a knife fighter. No one collects that many scars without having made it through a good number of fights.

The bespectacled man himself looked to be in his late thirties or possibly early forties. Either way, there was an experienced glint in his eye and mannerisms that was difficult to miss. Whoever that man was, he'd been through enough hell for it to have left its mark on him. After having been through more than his share of fire, Clint knew that mark all too well.

"I want you to get up, go to the next car and sit tight," Clint said in a quiet, calm voice.

"But the only other passenger car is that way," Bertolucci said as he nodded in the direction of the three men.

"You're not going that way. You're going the other way."

"That's the sleeper car. We didn't pay for a compartment there."

"Dammit, just do what I say," Clint snapped. "Otherwise, why the hell did you ask me to do this job?"

"Those are just sleeper compartments," the doctor explained. "They're locked unless you've paid for a key."

Clint let out an exasperated breath. "Are you sure about that?"

"Yes. I checked."

"And you didn't think to pay for a private compartment?"

Meekly, Bertolucci replied, "They were all booked."

"Fine. Just take this, then," Clint said as he drew the small .32 Colt New Line pistol that had been tucked under his gunbelt.

"You expect me to fight with you?"

"I expect you to defend yourself."

"But I'm not a gunman."

"And you're not helpless, either," Clint said forcefully, making sure he wasn't speaking loud enough to draw attention. "I'll be right back. If things look like they're getting bad, find someplace safe and stay there. If someone gets close enough to do you harm, protect yourself. Got it?"

Bertolucci nodded. "What about you?"

Clint smirked and stood up. "I'm just gonna have a little chat with those three."

Chapter Fourteen

Clint walked toward the front of the passenger car as Bertolucci stayed behind and sank down into his seat. The doctor pulled his jacket around him tightly as if that was enough to make him blend in with his surroundings altogether.

There were a good amount of other people on the train, most of which were either asleep, talking amongst themselves or staring out their window in a bored stupor. There were women and children among them, but most of them were clustered in one corner of the car. By the looks of them, they could have been one large family. Clint didn't concern himself with them apart from the fact that they seemed content to stay put for the moment.

The three men in Clint's sights spoke to each other in hushed tones. Most of the talking was done by the bespectacled man who cut his words off completely once Clint got close enough to hear them. As Clint drew closer, all three of the other men tensed up like bowstrings.

"What the hell do you want?" the bespectacled man asked in a voice that sounded like a fork being dragged across dry slate.

Clint took a few more steps, which was enough to give him some degree of privacy. Most of the other passengers in that car had already drifted away from the armed men. The few who remained were dead asleep.

Putting on a pleasant expression, Clint said, "Just thought I'd come and say hello."

"You said it," grunted the younger man with the scraggly hair.

"Seeing as how you three have been watching us so closely since we boarded this train," Clint said, "I thought you might have wanted to chat."

The younger man's face twisted into a snarl as he began to move forward. He was stopped by the back of the bespectacled man's hand as it slapped against his chest. Pushing the younger man back to his original spot, the bespectacled man locked eyes with Clint and said, "Actually, that may not be a bad idea. Let's start off with just who the hell you are?"

"I'm Clint Adams. Who are you?"

"I'm McPike," the bespectacled man said. Up close, he seemed even scrawnier than he had at a distance. Most of the bulk of his upper body came from the shirt, vest and jacket he wore. His cheeks were sunken just a bit and his hair was thinning on top to form something of a partial ring around the back of his head. His eyes, however, were sharp as razors and his voice had the edge of someone who was accustomed to being obeyed.

"This here is Sanders and Cosh," he added while nodding to the scraggly young man and the fellow with darker skin respectively. "Clint Adams, huh? Seems like the doc doesn't spare any expense when he hires a gun hand."

"He's just a little nervous about traveling by himself. Maybe he's not so crazy for feeling that way."

"He sure ain't," McPike said. "Do you know what you're helping that man haul on this train?"

"I've got a good idea. What business is it of yours?" Clint asked.

"It's more our business than it is yours."

"Maybe you should tell that to the man who came up with the original idea in the first place. It seems to me, that man is Doctor Bertolucci and he's not too wild about the fact that you three have decided to follow him onto this train."

McPike showed Clint a smirk that was even uglier than the scowl he'd been wearing before.

"I'm glad you came over here, Adams. Saves us the trouble of approaching you. There's money to be made in this matter and plenty of it can go to you."

"Is that a fact?" Clint asked with feigned wonder.

Ignoring the sarcasm dripping from Clint's tone, McPike said, "It is and you're in a prime position to earn more than enough to make it worth your while."

"Let me guess. All I need to do is sign up with you and I'll get my pay."

"You got it," McPike replied.

"Where do I start?" Clint asked. "By killing Bertolucci for you?"

"Nah. All you gotta do is step aside and let us have a word with him. We're not even supposed to hurt the little fella unless he does something stupid."

Suddenly, Clint couldn't help but think about the pistol he'd given to the doctor.

"Who's putting up this money you're offering?" Clint asked. "The railroad?"

"Not just one railroad company," McPike told him. "Damn near all of them. But that ain't even where the real profits are comin' from. That's comin' from some men who don't have a damn thing to do with the railroad."

"And who might they be?"

"Wouldn't you like to know?" Sanders growled.

Clint locked eyes with him and tersely replied, "Yes, I would. That's why I asked. You can either answer me or shut your goddamn mouth."

Sanders was taken aback by that. He recoiled instinctively from the fire in Clint's eyes but immediately tried to build up his wounded pride by bowing up again. "I'll say what I fucking please and if'n you don't like it . . ." he growled while slapping his hand against his holstered pistol.

"Easy," McPike warned through a smile that he wore like a shallow layer of cheap paint. "Now's not the time for that. Now's the time to make deals and maybe a few new friends. Isn't that right, Adams?"

"I haven't heard a deal worth taking yet," Clint said.

"You sign up with us and you get an equal share of what we're being paid."

The other two men didn't seem too happy about that, but weren't going to speak their minds just yet.

"How much are you talking about?" Clint asked.

McPike's eyes narrowed to study Clint carefully. "Four hundred now. Another five when the doctor and his cargo is delivered to where it needs to go."

"Which is where, exactly?"

"You in or out, Adams?" McPike snapped. "You've heard enough to make a decision."

After a few seconds, Clint replied, "Why don't I let you know?"

McPike shrugged. "Fine. You've got until this train pulls into its next station. Should be a few hours."

"Until then," Clint said while locking eyes with McPike, Sanders and Cosh in turn, "give us some room to breathe."

Holding his hands up to show they were empty, McPike stepped back. "Come on, boys," he said to the other two. "Let's see what's being served in the dining car."

Chapter Fifteen

McPike and his two partners backed away from Clint and left the passenger car without incident. Clint stood his ground waiting for the first hint of trouble until it seemed more like he was waiting for an excuse to draw his Colt and put it to work.

Turning away from the narrow door leading to the walkway connecting the passenger car to the dining car, Clint assessed the rest of the people in there with him. There was no reason to think those three men he'd spoken to were the only ones with their sights set on Bertolucci. If there were any others of that sort, however, they were doing a real good job of blending in. All Clint saw was the same mixture of anxiousness and boredom among the passengers.

Clint kept a friendly expression on his face as he made his way back to the spot where the doctor was waiting. He nodded at the few people who looked in his direction without lingering for too long in one spot. Clint had been concerned about being overheard while he and McPike were talking.

It wasn't so much a matter of anyone hearing a precious secret, but everything would be less complicated with fewer people knowing the details of what was happening with Bertolucci. All it took was a few overheard sentences passed along to the wrong person by another passenger and there was potentially another threat to worry about. As Clint walked through the car, however, the rattling of wheels upon the track and the shifting of the car itself put his concerns to rest. Other people were talking freely and he couldn't make out more than a few words of what they were saying. In fact, they had to raise their voices just to be heard by whoever was near them.

By the time he got back to Bertolucci's seat, Clint was feeling somewhat better. The doctor, on the other hand, was pale and dripping with sweat.

"Are they gone?" Bertolucci asked.

"For now," Clint told him as he sat down on the wooden bench.

"What do you mean? Are they gone or not?"

"It's a moving train," Clint said. "They went to another car, which is pretty much as far away as they can go for the moment."

"Who are they?"

"Does the name McPike sound familiar?"

Bertolucci thought about it and shrugged. "Not really."

"Strange, but it seems you have a good number of dangerous men after you and you don't know much about it."

"I knew they were after me," Bertolucci squeaked. "I never said I knew their names!"

"All right, fair enough," Clint said since he didn't pick up on any hint that the doctor was trying to slip any sort of lie past him. "Let's get you out of here."

Gripping his seat as if he was afraid of being tossed off the train altogether, Bertolucci asked, "What did you have in mind?"

"The next car over."

"You mean the one where those men went?"

"No," Clint said while getting up and grabbing the saddle-bags he'd brought on board with him. "I mean the sleeper car. Perhaps we can find one we can use or share."

"I told you, they're all booked."

"Then maybe we can pay someone a visit or at least see what's in the next car after that one. Wouldn't you rather take a look for ourselves instead of sitting here where those three men know where to find us when they're good and ready?"

Bertolucci contemplated that for all of two seconds before grabbing his small case and standing up. "I believe you've made your point," he said. "Let's go."

Clint opened the door leading out of the car and allowed Bertolucci to pass by him. After taking two steps in the doctor's wake, Clint felt the clubbing impact of something heavy knocking against the side of his head from above.

Chapter Sixteen

It happened the moment Clint stepped onto the balcony that was attached to the back of the passenger car. His boot had barely made contact with the metal grate when his head was knocked to one side and his ears were filled with the dull roar of swirling pain.

He staggered forward a couple of steps, one hand reaching up to his aching head and the other stretching out to grab whatever he could find. Right away, he touched the railing sectioning off the small exterior balcony and Clint stopped there.

Bertolucci was shouting something at him, but Clint couldn't hear anything over the commotion inside his skull.

The door slammed shut behind him with a jarring bang, which was followed by the heavy impact of something landing behind him. Clint spun around to find Cosh standing in front of the door. When Clint took a swing at the dark-skinned man, his balance was so off kilter that he managed to crack Bertolucci in the jaw instead. The doctor went straight down to sit on the balcony with his back against the railing.

As Cosh straightened up, Clint took a second to orient himself. His balance was still off and his ears were jangling, but he wasn't about to fall over. In fact, his swaying stance allowed him to look upward at just the right time to see Sanders crouching at the edge of the car's roof. At least now he could imagine how he'd been bushwhacked. With Cosh waiting in the same spot, it would have been easy for him to kick Clint in the head while jumping down.

There was a hint of surprise on Cosh's face when he saw Clint collect himself after being knocked in the head. That wore off quickly, however, and he lunged at Clint to hit him again. Clint leaned to one side to avoid the straight jab, which nearly sent him staggering over the edge of the railing altogether. He opened his arms wide to catch himself and caught hold of Cosh instead. Tightening his arms in a bear hug, Clint did the first thing he could think of and simply tried to squeeze the breath out of the other man.

For a moment, he thought his simple strategy was going to work. Cosh was caught off his guard so much that he gulped and gasped as if he truly was going to lose his breath. Instead, he snapped his head forward to crack it against Clint's face. That wasn't enough to break Clint's grip, but it loosened his arms enough for Cosh to free one arm of his own. The first thing he did was reach for the gun at his side.

Clint may have still been a little wobbly, but he knew it wouldn't take long for Cosh to draw his pistol. And even if he could put that off for a bit, there was still another man with the advantage of higher ground to worry about. The more Clint tried to wrangle Cosh, the easier it would be for the other man to slip free.

Before he lost what little advantage he did have over Cosh, Clint lifted him off his feet and heaved him over the top of the railing. Cosh was already starting to cry out when Clint released his grip. After that, the only sound Cosh made was when he slapped against the side of the train before toppling to the ground.

Without taking a moment to catch his breath, Clint set his sights upward to where Sanders was perched on the edge of the train's roof. Sanders looked at the spot where his partner had just been, his eyes wide in a mix of surprise and horror. Those were quickly washed away by rage as he pointed his pistol down at the balcony and pulled his trigger.

The gun barked once, sending a bullet down past Clint to spark against the grating near his boot. Clint jumped up to grab the edge of the roof with one hand to give himself a boost as he jumped up and reached for Sanders with his other hand. He grabbed hold of Sanders by the ankle and pulled him down with one quick tug.

Sanders hit the edge of the roof on his backside, knocking the gun from his hand, and slid the rest of the way down. Landing directly in front of Clint, he was assaulted by two straight punches to the nose before he could get his bearings. Blood streaming down his face, he grabbed Clint's shoulders and started driving his knee into Clint's midsection with every bit of strength he had.

The first knee caught Clint in the hip and didn't do much damage. The second blow pounded slightly above his groin and forced a good amount of wind from his sails. Clint shoved him back and sent a powerful uppercut deep into Sanders's gut. The younger man had a muscular body that absorbed most of the impact. Rather than continue trading punches, Sanders reached for his side.

It wasn't until then that Clint saw the gunbelt around Sanders's waist was a double rig. Before the young man could get to his second pistol, Clint drew his Colt, jammed its barrel into Saunders's chest and pulled his trigger. A muffled thump lifted Sanders from his feet and the second caused his entire body to go limp. Before he could crumple onto the balcony, Clint shoved him back so he could fall off the train and be left behind in its dust.

Keeping his Colt in hand, Clint waited for the next attack. When it didn't come, he holstered the pistol so he could grab hold of the edge of the train's roof. "Wait here," he said to Bertolucci.

"S-sure," the doctor squeaked. "That's f-f-fine with me."

Chapter Seventeen

When Clint pulled himself up, he fully expected to be the target in a shooting gallery. No bullets came hissing in his direction, though, which was only a small relief. He hoisted himself up again to take a longer look and even got all the way on top of the train without a hitch. Even though he didn't particularly enjoy being shot at, Clint would have at least known where the remaining gunman was.

McPike was still around and since he wasn't showing his face just yet, it meant he was biding his time until another chance presented itself. Just to be certain, Clint walked the entire length of the passenger car's roof with Colt in hand. The only thing up there was a whole lot of wind so he made his way back to the end where he'd started.

The first thing Clint saw when he jumped down to the balcony between cars was a frightened doctor pointing a .32 at him.

"Oh!" Bertolucci said. "It's you."

"Yes, it's me," Clint replied. "Could you lower the gun now?"

"Oh, certainly."

As soon as the pistol was no longer being aimed at him, Clint took it away from Bertolucci. Since the doctor wasn't eager to hang on to the weapon, he was more than happy to be rid of it.

"Did you . . . dispatch the third of those men?" Bertolucci asked.

"He wasn't up there."

"Where did he go?"

Clint didn't answer right away. He took hold of the door handle and opened it just far enough, so he could take a peek inside the passenger car. More of the people inside were milling around, but none of them seemed to be particularly rattled by the commotion that had taken place. Considering how noisy it was inside that wooden box, Clint wasn't surprised. In fact, one of the small children had started wailing loud enough to drown out an entire firing line.

"I asked you a question!" the doctor blustered.

Suddenly, the door to the car connected to the passenger car was opened and a uniformed man filled the entrance.

"Is there a problem out here?"

It was a good thing Bertolucci was no longer armed because he twitched hard enough in surprise that he might have fired a shot at the conductor without even thinking about it. Before the doctor could give one of his stammering responses, Clint shook his head.

"No problem," he said. "Why?"

"I thought I heard gunshots, that's why," the conductor said while glaring at both men on the balcony.

Clint nodded and patted his holster. "My friend here expressed some interest in buying my pistol, so he insisted on seeing it in action."

"So you decided to fire it out here?"

"Yeah. More or less."

75

The conductor was a burly man sporting a thick mustache that made him look even more like a walrus. The skin around his eyes formed a series of deep wrinkles when he scowled at Clint. One furry eyebrow raised a bit when he looked over to Bertolucci and asked, "Something wrong with him?"

"He's just not used to the kick of a real firearm," Clint chuckled.

The conductor scowled again and stepped outside. Although he didn't wear a weapon in plain sight, that didn't mean he wasn't keeping one stashed where he could get to it if the need arose. After shutting the door behind him, he said, "Hand it over."

Clint weighed his options in the space of a second. Figuring he stood a better chance of talking his way out of a situation instead of trying to fight a man who was just doing his job, he removed the Colt from its holster and held it so its handle was pointed toward the uniformed man.

The conductor wrapped his fingers around the Colt's grip so he could heft its weight. Stretching his arm out to point the barrel over the side of the balcony, he took a long look along the top of the pistol. "It's got good balance," he said while nodding in approval.

"Damn right it does," Clint replied.

"Looks to have been tinkered with a bit."

"Modified it myself."

Glancing toward Clint, the conductor asked, "May I?"

"Be my guest."

Taking aim at a tree roughly twenty yards away from the tracks, the conductor squeezed the Colt's trigger to send a small bunch of leaves fluttering into the air. Turning the Colt over to look at both sides, the conductor nodded some more.

"It sure does have some kick to it."

"That's what I tried to tell him," Clint said as he motioned toward Bertolucci.

The doctor showed him a shaky smile and nodded.

"Tell you what," the conductor said, "if this is too much gun for that fella there, I'll make an offer."

"Actually, I think we've agreed on a price that'll do just fine. Isn't that right?"

"Y-yes! I was first to make the offer," Bertolucci said with just a bit too much enthusiasm.

The conductor was still too busy inspecting the Colt to take much notice of the other man's nervousness. With a heavy sigh, he handed the pistol back to Clint.

"It's a shame. That's a damn fine piece of weaponry."

"Thank you kindly," Clint said as he took the pistol back. "By the way, are there any open sleeper compartments in that car? The other one was getting a bit noisy."

"That kid screaming again?" the conductor groaned. "I've got one of the smaller ones free, but there ain't a lot of room."

"How much is it?"

"Let me fire off a few more shots and I'll let you have it for nothin'," the burly man said with a sly wink.

Clint slipped a few fresh rounds into the cylinder and snapped it shut. "Have at it, friend!"

The conductor picked a few more targets out at random and spent the rounds in a single string of sharp bangs. Bertolucci flinched at every one of them as if each bullet caught him in the chest.

Handing back the Colt, the conductor tipped his hat and crossed to the passenger car. "Gotta check on the folks in here. Nice talkin' to ya."

Chapter Eighteen

"When that conductor said there wasn't a lot of room," Clint grunted, "he wasn't kidding."

The compartment was barely more than a large cupboard that was tall enough to contain a pair of bunks stacked one on top of the other and was just deep enough for someone to lay on their back while stretching out. It was separated from the single aisle running the length of the car by a thick, dark blue curtain.

Inside the compartment, Clint lay on his side upon the bottom bunk while Bertolucci curled up on the top one.

"Will you sit still?" Clint snapped.

"I can't get comfortable on this blasted board! Are you certain this is better than the bench or even sitting on the floor?"

"We're out of sight in here at least," Clint replied. "And it's probably best if we stay that way for a little while. At least until McPike cools down after losing his two partners."

"You think he was angry?"

"I'd say it's fifty-fifty. On one hand, he might know those two like brothers and would want to tear apart anyone who harmed them. On the other hand, he could have just hired them for a job and doesn't give a shit if they live or die so long as the job gets done."

"Either way, he'd still want to see us dead," Bertolucci pointed out.

"Which is why we're in here."

"Hiding."

"What did you just say?" Clint asked.

"I said we're hiding. Isn't that what we're doing?"

Clint climbed off his bunk, pulled open the curtain and stood so he was looking straight at the upper bunk. Before saying another word, he checked behind the curtain directly across from him. Just as it had been when he'd checked as they'd first arrived in that car, the bunks behind that curtain were occupied by two old men who were sleeping so soundly they might as well have been dead.

"You have any better ideas?" Clint snapped.

Bertolucci blinked and shook his head. "No. Did I say something to offend you?"

"You damn near called me a coward!"

"Not at all! I merely pointed out that we're hiding. Apparently, you're not a man who's accustomed to such a thing. I, on the other hand, have had a great deal of practice at it."

"Been on the run a long time, have you?"

"Ever since my second week of school," Bertolucci said. "That's how long it took for the larger boys to form into a pack of wolves and start preying on the smaller ones. I was the smallest and youngest because I was also the smartest, which was why I was in school at such an early age. The beatings weren't life threatening, but they were consistent. I was too slow to outrun them, so I developed a talent for hiding. I'm used to it, you see."

"Well, I hate it," Clint growled.

"Probably just as much as I hate having to hire someone like you to keep me alive."

"Someone like me?"

"Yes. A man's supposed to take care of himself, right? For a man to admit that's not the case is quite a blow sometimes. But a man like you probably doesn't know so much about that."

And here Clint was about to get mad at the thought that Bertolucci considered him to be just a hired killer. Seeing the hints of admiration in the doctor's eyes was enough to put out the angry fires smoldering in Clint's belly.

"Hiding's not easy for any man," he said. "Neither is running, but sometimes it's gotta be done."

"Just so long as we don't make a habit of it, yes?" Bertolucci asked.

"Damn right."

Chapter Nineteen

Bertolucci stayed in his bunk for a good portion of the rest of the train ride. Granted, Clint did ask him to stay put and out of sight whenever possible, but the doctor had no qualms with following that particular order when it was given. Considering what Bertolucci had seen when McPike's two partners dropped down on them outside the passenger car, Clint couldn't exactly blame him for wanting to keep his head down.

As far as McPike was concerned, Clint didn't see hide nor hair of him again. For a while, Clint figured the bespectacled man would seek him out to take at least one more shot at Bertolucci. The more time that passed without another ambush, the more concerned Clint became.

The conductor strolled down the aisle cutting through the middle of the sleeper car, shouting out the name of their next stop. Clint was sitting on the edge of his bunk, legs dangling over the side of his cot, as the bulky man ambled past.

"How much farther until Galveston?" Clint asked.

"It's two stops after this one," the conductor told him.

"Any problem with me getting into the baggage compartments?"

Hearing that brought the conductor to a stop. Furrowing his brow, he asked, "Why'd you want to do something like that?"

"I left something in my bags that I need."

"Is it important?"

"Yes!" Bertolucci interjected.

"How important is it?"

"It's my medicine and eyeglasses. Not having them when I need them is making me feel quite ill." Pressing his hands against his belly, the doctor added, "My head is quite achy without my glasses and my medicine is for a condition I have that affects my digestion. Not a good combination to be without, I'm afraid."

The conductor waited until Bertolucci was finished talking before blinking once and shifting his gaze over to Clint. "How important is it?"

Having picked up on the conductor's tone the first time he'd asked his question, Clint already had a bit of money in hand by the time that question was asked to him. Clint handed over the money, which brought much more of a response from the conductor than Bertolucci's rambling explanation.

"Well now," the conductor said as he tucked the money away into one of his uniform's pockets, "I can see this is a pressing matter. Since the comfort of our passengers is my greatest concern, I think I can take you into the baggage compartment."

"You can just get me in," Clint said. "No need to waste your time watching me sift through our things."

The conductor cleared his throat and put an uncomfortable expression onto his face. Amazingly enough, his discomfort vanished once he was given a bit of extra cash to go along with the first bribe.

"Come on," Clint said, as the conductor motioned for Clint to follow him toward the other end of the car.

Bertolucci hung his legs over the side of his bunk, but went no further. "Are you sure?"

"Yeah, come on."

"But . . . what if there's…trouble?"

"Won't be no trouble," the conductor said from the far end of the aisle. "I'll vouch for ya."

Bertolucci kept his eyes on Clint.

"Would you rather take your chances on there being trouble here?" Clint asked. "While I'm away?"

After a second or two, Bertolucci jumped down. When his feet hit the floor, the little .32 he'd been given back fell from his pocket and landed by his feet. He tried to scoop it up, but dropped it again before finally grabbing the pistol and hiding it away.

"Jumpy little fella, ain't he?" the conductor mused.

Clint nodded. "You have no idea."

Chapter Twenty

The baggage compartment was just a section of the livery car, separated by a thin wooden wall and a door that was flimsy enough to be knocked off its hinges on accident. After showing the men inside, the conductor motioned toward the stables where Eclipse and a pair of other horses were being kept.

"There's the bags," he said, waving to several neat piles of saddlebags, carpetbags and valises. "No matter how much you paid to get in here, I can't have you stealing from any of the other folks on this train. I find out anything's missing, I'll find you and tan both yer hides."

"What we need is in there," Clint said as he pointed to the wall with the flimsy door in it.

Sighing, the conductor used one of the many keys jangling from a ring on his belt to unlock the narrow door built into the wooden partition. Even before he turned the key in the lock, the door swung open.

"Aw hell," the conductor sighed.

"What?" Bertolucci snapped. "What's wrong?"

"This damn door ain't worth the wood it's made out of," the conductor said. "Always coming unlocked and even when it does work properly, someone's leaving it open."

"You mind giving us a minute?" Clint asked.

"Sure, why not?" the conductor said as he put his keys away. "Pull it shut when you're through. And remember, if something comes up stolen . . ."

"I remember," Clint said. "Thanks."

The conductor was still grumbling to himself as he walked out of the car. After the door slammed shut behind him, his muffled complaining could still be heard.

"I think he's waiting out there for us," Bertolucci whispered.

Clint studied the contents of the small room behind the flimsy door. "Good. We won't take long. How many boxes did we load onto this train?"

"Seven, I believe."

"God damn it."

Bertolucci looked in the room. Apart from a small strongbox that was bolted to the floor and locked tighter than the Federal Reserve, there were half a dozen narrow wooden crates stacked neatly in the corner.

"But," the doctor gulped, "there's only six."

Clint walked over to the stack and hunkered down to place both hands on either side of one of the crates. Knowing all too well how heavy they were, he carefully lifted one while letting out a labored breath. It wasn't impossible to bring the crate up, but it was far from easy.

"You think we should move them?" Bertolucci asked.

Clint ignored the doctor as he set the crate down and stepped out of the small room. From there, he looked around at the rest of the livery car, paying special attention to the floor. When he got to the horse stalls, he found something that caught his eye.

Crouching down, Clint swept away some stray bits of straw to fully expose a deep gouge that had been made in the floorboards. Clint looked up to find Eclipse looking right back down at him from his stall.

"What happened, boy?" Clint wondered out loud. "Did you give him a fright?"

The Darley Arabian let out a huffing breath and shook a fly off his ear.

Bertolucci started to ask another question, but stopped after a few words when Clint silenced him with a sharply raised finger pointed in his direction. Rather than press the matter, the doctor kept quiet and watched as Clint continued to poke around.

Making his way to the last stall in the short row, Clint tested the gate and found it to be open. Since there wasn't an animal in that stall, that wasn't much of a surprise. Clint merely had to sweep his feet in wide arcs in front of him as he walked around the stall, however, to find something that was much more interesting.

Bertolucci leaned over the low divider at the front of the stall. "What's that?" he asked, his eyes locked on an object that had been hidden beneath a pile of loose hay and a horse blanket.

"Why don't you tell me?" Clint replied as he exposed another one of the small crates that had been loaded from Bertolucci's cart.

Clint had never seen the doctor move so quickly as he did when he rushed into the stall to get to that box. Dropping to his knees, Bertolucci inspected the box and immediately made his first discovery.

"It's open," he said.

"Check inside," Clint told him.

Carefully removing the lid, Bertolucci looked inside the box. "Oh no," he said as his hands reached in to touch the strips of iron that had been specially crafted by Kurt Ferguson. "There are two pieces missing."

"Only two?" Clint said. "That's not so bad."

"You don't understand. That's enough to . . ."

"To what?" Clint urged.

"Enough to see how it was made so my process might be copied." After carefully replacing the lid, Bertolucci stood up and then attempted to pick up the crate. After grunting a few times, he managed to lift the crate off the floor. "This-isn't-this isn't a good . . ."

Before the doctor hurt himself, Clint took the crate from him and started carrying it back to the room where the rest of them were being kept.

"This isn't a good thing," Bertolucci continued. "In fact, it's quite bad."

"Could have been a whole lot worse," Clint pointed out.

"Yes, but the ore is just a piece of my innovation. In the wrong hands, it could lead to shoddy craftsmanship and even damage to the trains I'm trying to help. Too much of that sort of thing and no railroad will want to risk dealing with anything I have to offer."

"Maybe that was the point of this robbery," Clint said. Shaking his head, he cussed under his breath. "I shouldn't have allowed this to happen."

Both men looked down at the now complete stack of crates. Placing a hand on Clint's shoulder, Bertolucci said,

"You didn't allow this to happen. You were concerned with guarding me and I cannot fault you for that."

"I was hoping you wouldn't knock off some of my pay for this job," Clint said with a grin.

"Now that, we might have to discuss."

Chapter Twenty-One

McPike wasn't seen or heard from during the rest of the train ride. After a while, Clint became convinced that the gunman had either gotten what he'd wanted after using his two partners as a distraction or taken what he could get after Sanders and Cosh had been tossed off the train. Either way, the bespectacled man wasn't a problem for the duration of the ride.

As they drew closer to Galveston, the air blowing in through the windows became saltier and cooler as it blew in from the Gulf of Mexico. He and Bertolucci spent most of their time in the livery car so they could watch the cargo while Clint kept an eye on the doctor. Since the sleeper compartment they'd been using was now free to be rented to someone else, the conductor didn't have much of a problem with the arrangement.

Every so often, Clint and Bertolucci would venture out to stretch their legs or get something to eat. When the livery car was opened during a stop, Clint made himself useful by helping to unload a horse or help get another one onboard. When the train finally pulled into the station near Galveston, Clint felt like he should get a paycheck from the railroad. Instead, he waved goodbye to the conductor after taking off the last of the crates and led Eclipse back onto solid ground.

There was a hand cart waiting for them at the station. Bertolucci helped a bit with loading it. Once Eclipse was saddled and Clint sat astride the Darley Arabian, Bertolucci was waiting by the cart with his hands folded patiently.

"Well," Clint said. "Let's go."

"Not just yet," Bertolucci replied.

"Look, McPike probably got off that train some time ago, but let's not push our luck."

Bertolucci looked past Clint and said, "All right. Now we can get moving."

Clint looked in the direction that the doctor had been watching and saw a young woman hurrying toward the cart. She looked to be somewhere in her early twenties with long, dark brown hair pulled back into a thick tail that hung down to the small of her back. Her skin had a slight olive hue and her lips were a full, natural red.

"Welcome back, Carmine," the young woman said. Her eyes quickly darted over to Clint as a slight flush colored her cheeks. "Who's this?"

"This is Clint Adams," Bertolucci said. "I've hired him to work with us."

Her eyes widened as she asked, "Is he another scientist?"

"No, but he is a kind of specialist in his own right."

It didn't take long for the woman's eyes to drift toward the holster strapped to Clint's side. Almost immediately, the excitement that had been there before left her face and she furrowed her brow skeptically.

"Can I have a word with you, Carmine?" she asked.

"Of course!"

"Alone," she quickly added.

"Oh . . ."

"It's all right," Clint said before the doctor was forced to struggle for his next words. "I'll make sure everything is ready to go. That is . . . unless you planned on having me carry these crates?"

"There's a buckboard over there," the young woman said, pointing in the direction from which she'd come.

Clint looked over that way to find a buckboard that was slightly larger than the wagon Bertolucci had used before boarding the train. Since there were no other buckboards in that vicinity, Clint started leading Eclipse over that way. When he drew closer to the woman, he tipped his hat and offered his hand. "I'm Clint."

"So I've heard," she snipped.

"Don't be rude!" Bertolucci said curtly as he walked over to her. Positioning himself between the other two, he said, "Clint Adams, this is Antonia Hoffs. She's my assistant."

Antonia took Clint's hand and shook it as though she was afraid of catching something from him.

"Pleased to meet you," Clint said, more as a test to see if she would return the courtesy.

She didn't.

As Bertolucci and Antonia moved away from Clint so they could talk privately, Clint took the handcart over to the buckboard. The train was already pulling out, so with no manpower to help him, Clint actually used Eclipse to help him push it.

He started loading the crates one at a time, being careful to handle each one carefully in the process. Every so often, a young man or enterprising kid would rush up to him and offer to help with the chore for a fee. As much as he wanted to lighten his workload, Clint refused the offer and continued with the task himself. The last thing he needed was one of those crates being dropped by a pair of hurried hands.

As he worked, Clint watched the animated discussion going on between Bertolucci and his assistant. He didn't need to hear what they were saying to know that the attractive young woman wasn't happy about Clint being with them. Bertolucci was doing his best to defend Clint, but wasn't making a lot of progress in changing Antonia's mind.

It was going to take a lot more work than a simple conversation for her to warm up to him, but Clint was looking forward to the challenge.

Chapter Twenty-Two

Sometime later, Clint was driving the buckboard down a wide trail heading due south toward a wide expanse of water in the distance. What he saw was the Gulf of Mexico and it always somehow managed to seem close enough to touch while remaining just out of reach.

"Beautiful, isn't it?" Clint mused.

There was no response from anyone else in the buckboard with him. Antonia sat on the seat beside Clint while Bertolucci was in the back fussing with each crate to make sure it hadn't been tampered with during the train ride.

Clint shifted around to look behind him and then faced forward again. Knowing Bertolucci was too distracted for conversation, he glanced over to Antonia.

"Must be nice living so close to the Gulf. It's been a while since I've seen much more than desert or prairie."

"It's nice," she replied with a shrug.

"How long of a ride is it before we reach the doctor's laboratory?"

"There's a ways to go."

"Is it close to the water?" Clint asked.

"Very close," Antonia scoffed. "It's on an island, you know."

"Oh, that's right."

"I know it is."

Clint pulled in a deep breath and let it out with a measured sigh. "So, is this how it's going to be?"

"What do you mean?"

Pulling back on his reins, Clint brought the wagon to a stop amid the scraping of hooves against the ground. Eclipse was tied to the cart so he could walk alongside, which allowed the stallion to adjust to the change a little easier.

"You can think what you want about me," Clint said, "but don't think I'm an idiot. I'm also not blind."

"Well, those are good things."

"There might be more good where that came from, but you won't know if you keep treating me like I'm some kind of . . ."

"Killer?" she offered.

"I was going to say leper, but that'll do. To tell the truth, I'm not too happy about either one."

Antonia shrugged, crossed her arms and stared straight ahead.

"I'm sure the doc told you I wasn't just some hired gun," Clint said.

Antonia kept staring.

"He told you that, right?"

Eventually, she replied, "Yes."

"From the sound of it, you need some protection anyway," Clint offered.

"Perhaps we wouldn't if Carmine didn't insist on stooping to the level of those who are trying to steal from us."

Suddenly, Bertolucci looked up from what he'd been doing. "Have we stopped? Why have we stopped? Are we there?"

Clint snapped his reins to get the team moving again. When Eclipse felt the tug on his reins, the stallion started moving as well. That was all the incentive Bertolucci needed to get back to inspecting the ore contained in those crates.

"So," Clint said, "you think that shooting begets more shooting?"

"Something like that," Antonia replied.

"And, by that way of thinking, if nobody owned a gun there wouldn't be any more fighting. Or wars, for that matter?"

"I'm not stupid either, Mister Adams," she sneered, finally looking over at Clint instead of merely acknowledging him with the occasional sideways glance. "I realize that it is necessary for someone to protect themselves. In fact, as a woman, I'd say that there are more people trying to hurt me than those hurting a man."

"Some might say that's offensive to women," Clint pointed out.

"And I'd say that those people have never been raped."

"Oh, I'm sorry."

Antonia lowered her head and looked over at Clint again. "All I'm saying is that men are always trying to hurt each other and they try to hurt women in even more ways."

"Have you ever been . . ."

"No," Antonia said. "Thank God. I was just trying to make a point. My original point is that more trouble is caused by guns that is solved by them."

"In a perfect world, you'd be absolutely right. Unfortunately, we're not in a perfect world."

"You sound just like Carmine."

"What?" Bertolucci called from the back.

"Nothing," Antonia sighed. "We're just talking."

"Oh, wonderful! I knew you two would get along!" After that, Bertolucci lost himself once again in whatever he was doing.

"I don't intend on causing trouble," Clint said. "If that's what you're worried about. My job is just to help out when trouble does come your way."

"See, that's the problem. As long as there are men with guns strutting around there's always going to be trouble. Once that's no longer how things are, we can finally stop trying to prove who's better in a fight and get some real work done."

"True," Clint said. "But in order for things to go your way, everyone would have to give up their guns."

"And what's wrong with that?"

"Nothing, except it won't happen. Also, it shouldn't happen."

Antonia's expression made it look as though she'd just been forced to chew on a lemon. "What kind of thing is that to say?"

"It's the truth. Guns aren't going to be abandoned and they shouldn't be."

"Why not?"

"Because they're tools, plain and simple," Clint said. "The fact that we make tools is what separates us from the rest of the animals."

"So you at least agree we're animals?" Antonia asked slyly.

"Of course! Anyone with a working pair of eyes could tell you that much."

Antonia smirked, but caught herself before it grew into a full smile. Seeing that he was making a bit of progress with her, Clint leaned over just enough to nudge her with his elbow and say, "So tell me something else you hate about me."

"What?"

"It makes the time go by faster."

"I don't hate you, Mister Adams," she admitted.

"Call me Clint."

"I don't hate you, Clint. I just don't appreciate men who have to prove themselves by hurting others."

"I can see how that might ruffle the feathers of someone who works in the name of science."

"Yes!" she said, perhaps not realizing how vigorously she was agreeing with him. "It's like the work I hope to do and the work that Carmine does is to build something up."

"And then along comes some bunch of loudmouth cowboys to knock it down," Clint said before she could.

Now Antonia looked over to him and kept her eyes on him. "That's it exactly. In a figurative sense, of course."

"Of course."

Antonia pulled her wrap around her a bit tighter. The further south they rode, the closer they got to the Gulf and the cooler each breeze became. As she shifted her weight, Antonia managed to scoot a few inches closer to Clint as well.

"I see it all the time," she said.

"What do you see?" Clint asked.

"Men with guns. Especially in Texas."

"Let me guess. You're not from Texas."

"How did you know?"

"Lucky guess," Clint chuckled. "You strike me as someone from the east. New York, maybe?"

"Maryland."

"Did you go to school there?"

"As much as I could. My father and uncle were professors, so they taught me once I couldn't go any farther at a university. They had some connections to get me into a class or two, but it just became easier for them to do it themselves. They taught me a lot."

"I bet."

"My uncle introduced me to Carmine," she continued. "And when I came out here to help him, I see so much wide open beautiful country that's just swarming with armed men and savages."

"Some of those savages aren't so bad," Clint pointed out. "If you give them a chance, that is."

"That's exactly what I wanted to say when I started this whole thing. When people carry guns, it puts others on their guard. When people are on their guard, they're not as apt to talk to each other. Take those people right there, for example. If meeting an armed stranger wasn't so likely, they might be more apt to stop and talk to us or possibly offer a hand."

"People talk more than enough," Clint said. "And every so often, they say something useful."

"They'd say more if they weren't afraid."

"Being a little afraid isn't a bad thing," Clint said. "Keeps people from making stupid mistakes."

"Then perhaps we should talk to those people out there to ask their opinion on the matter," Antonia continued. "But we won't, of course, because we're concerned they might be armed. Actually, we know they'll be armed, so we're worried about them wanting to shoot us."

While Antonia concerned herself with the point she was trying to make, Clint focused on the people in the distance that she'd recently pointed out to him. There were four riders on horseback coming down the trail straight toward them. Since Clint hadn't seen them before, they must have either been off the trail somewhere or around a bend and out of sight. They were coming at them now, however, and they were coming fast.

"Do you know those people?" Clint asked, keeping his eyes fixed on the trail ahead.

Antonia looked that way as well and shook her head. "No. I was just making a point."

"Is there a town up ahead?"

"Not for a few miles."

"And there's not one behind us for a lot longer than that," Clint said. "That means there's no good reason for them to be charging at us that fast."

Chapter Twenty-Three

"Do you think they're bandits?" Antonia asked nervously.

"I don't know," Clint replied while squinting into the distance. "Maybe we can talk to them and find out. Do you think they're armed?"

Antonia started to say something, but quickly realized that Clint was just trying to get her riled up. Despite her best efforts, it worked.

"Maybe they're just in a hurry," she offered.

Clint set his reins down so he could keep them in place with his foot. That way, he had both hands free to double check that his Colt was fully loaded.

"Yeah," he said. "Maybe."

"Don't start any trouble. They could just be passing by."

"I know that. Any trouble that's gonna happen won't be started by me."

Snapping his head up from what he was doing, Bertolucci said, "Trouble? What trouble? Where?"

"Straight ahead," Clint told him. "Just try to keep your head down."

After all he'd been through so far, Bertolucci didn't need to be convinced any further to heed Clint's advice. In fact, when Antonia started to ask another question, the doctor reached out to grab her arm and pull her down to join him in the back of the cart.

"Do you keep a rifle on this cart?" Clint asked.

"No," Bertolucci replied, "but I've been meaning to rectify that."

"Where's that pistol I gave you?"

"The doctor does not carry a weapon," Antonia said in an uppity tone.

"Here it is," Bertolucci said as he handed over the little .32 Clint had lent him on the train.

Feeling that pistol's weight in his hand made Clint feel a little better. Not only was he slightly better armed than he'd been a moment ago, but Antonia was forced to eat the condescending words she'd all but spat at him. Seeing that the .32 was fully loaded as well, Clint tucked it under his gunbelt where he could get to it quickly if the need arose.

A shot cracked through the air, sending a bullet that hissed several feet away from Clint's head.

"What do you think, Antonia?" Clint shouted over his shoulder. "Still want to converse with these gentlemen?"

"Just shut up and shoot back!" she cried.

Clint smirked, allowing a few more seconds to pass so some of the distance between the buckboard and the approaching riders could be lessened. He didn't worry about returning fire right away, even though the men on horseback were firing more and more. Clint was content to line up his shots and wait for his targets to put themselves in range. As soon as that happened, he straightened his arm out, pointed and squeezed his trigger.

The Colt spat its round along with a plume of smoke. Clint watched as one of the horsemen fell straight back and rolled out of his saddle. His body hit the ground in a heap, flopped over and didn't move again.

As the horses got closer, Clint could see a bit more of the men riding them. Two of them carried rifles and rode with enough confidence to fire them properly while staying upright in the saddle. The third gripped his reins in one hand while firing a pistol with the other and leaning forward to stay low.

Clint fired once at the closest rifleman. The buckboard hit a bump in the road at that moment, affecting his shot, but got close enough to keep that man from firing right away, which was enough to buy Clint enough time to wedge himself down near the footboard where there was some slight bit of cover. It was far from comfortable, but Clint could lay most of the way down and occasionally sit up to get a better look at what was coming. Fortunately, the ambush had come while the buckboard was in the middle of an open stretch of trail so Clint didn't need to worry too much about steering the team.

More rifle shots burned through the air, some of them chipping off small portions of the buckboard. Clint laid as flat as he could, gauging the distance of the riders by the sound of their shots. Once he figured they were close enough, Clint sat up and took quick shots.

One of the riflemen was directly in front of Clint when he swung his Colt around to fire. Clint shot that one as if he was pointing his finger at the ambusher and knocked him from his saddle with two quick shots. The second rifleman was hanging back a short ways, almost directly behind the first. When the man who'd just been shot fell from his horse, he landed in front of the remaining rifleman and caused that man's horse to veer sharply to avoid being tripped up.

The sound of thundering hooves was behind Clint, so he twisted around to find the man with the pistol closing in on the cart. That man got so close that he was able to jump from his saddle and onto the buckboard. He jostled the cart as Clint fired at him once, causing him to miss. Clint hurried to get to his feet as the buckboard was boarded.

The attacker's face was filthy and covered in scars. Clint didn't recognize the son of a bitch, but also wasn't going to waste a lot of time in studying his features. Instead, he punched the ambusher in the face as hard as he could. The other man took the blow without much reaction, following up with a punch to Clint's stomach. The impact caused Clint's knees to buckle while robbing him of his next breath.

Before he could get his bearings again, Clint was teetering backward. There wasn't any room to maneuver, which meant Clint was falling onto the driver's seat before he could do anything about it. Clint fired once as he hit the seat on his side, but his bullet sailed into empty air. It was all he could do to hold onto his gun.

The gunman's eyes fixed on Clint as his finger tightened around his trigger. Clint had landed in a tangle of limbs, which made it that much harder for him to bring his gun around to take a shot.

Instead of gunfire, the next thing Clint heard was the dull thump of something solid hitting its mark. The gunman buckled and cursed in a snarling breath, giving Clint the precious couple of seconds he needed. The modified Colt barked once, drilling a hole through the gunman's heart and sending him straight off the side of the buckboard.

Clint turned slightly and saw Antonia kneeling near the side of the buckboard with one of the heavy strips of ore in her hands. She wielded the iron like a club as if she might have to use it again to dispatch another attacker.

"Thanks," Clint said as he holstered the Colt and sat in the driver's seat properly again.

She lowered her makeshift weapon and dropped back down into the buckboard to land on her backside.

Chapter Twenty-Four

"Wake up."

A wind blew that still smelled vaguely of gun smoke and dried blood.

There was movement in the near distance, most of which was horses shifting their weight and taking a breather after dragging a cart for most of the day.

A man lay on the ground, his left leg skewed at an unnatural angle and two large gashes opened in his face. Dirt and bits of gravel were stuck to the open wounds, only some of which fell loose when he lifted his head and tried to sit up. Almost immediately, he winced in pain and collapsed back down again.

"Open your eyes and look at me."

The man on the ground turned his head toward the sound of the voice coming from above him. When he didn't open his eyes, he felt something rough press down onto his mangled leg.

"Ow! Jesus!" the wounded man howled.

His eyes snapped open, focusing on the man looming over him. Clint glowered down at the wounded man, standing with one foot resting lightly on the other guy's leg. The slightest bit of pressure caused the wounded man to writhe and squirm like a worm on a hook.

"I'm not much of one for torture," Clint said, "but since we're in a bit of a rush and you fellas did decide to open fire on us first, I can make an exception."

"Wh-what do you want?" the wounded man groaned.

"Tell me what you were after."

"Fuck you!"

"Being nice to me is the only thing that'll get you to a doctor," Clint said.

"Ain't no doctor out here," the gunman sighed.

"There's one right over there," Clint said as he pointed to the buckboard. "But it might take some convincing to get him to help you, since you shot at him and all. Letting us know who sent you and what you want might go a ways in that direction, though."

When the gunman spat on the ground near Clint's boot, Clint responded by stepping on the man's knee.

"All right, all right!" the gunman wailed. "We were supposed to get the cargo you're hauling in that wagon."

"Who sent you?"

"Man by the name of—"

"What's going on here?" Bertolucci said as he hurried over to the spot where Clint was having his conversation. When he saw the gunman's predicament, Bertolucci said, "Stand back. I can help this man."

"Just a minute, doc," Clint said. "He was just about to tell me who hired these men to try and kill us."

Although Bertolucci was eager to help, being reminded of what had just happened made him more willing to give Clint some freedom to proceed as he wished.

"Who sent you?" Clint asked.

"Anthony Holland."

Looking over to Bertolucci, Clint asked, "You recognize that name?"

"There were several men who wanted to buy my notes and materials," the doctor replied. "I think that was one of them."

"What does this Holland fella want with the doctor here?" Clint asked.

"Get me some whiskey and a bed and I'll tell you all you wanna know," the gunman croaked.

Clint took his foot off of the gunman's leg and stepped back. "I'll get you something to drink, but you've got to talk if you want to leave this spot."

"Fine. Just make it quick. This hurts mighty bad."

"I've got a flask in my saddlebag," Clint said. "I've been keeping it lately for cold nights or rainy weather. Don't let him move and don't help him until I get back."

Bertolucci and Antonia kept their distance. As soon as Clint made it over to where Eclipse and the wagon had been parked, Antonia took a few tentative steps closer to the wounded man.

"Why did you want to shoot us?" she asked.

"You know damn well why," the wounded man replied.

"Who's Anthony Holland?"

The wounded man croaked out a few breaths, strained to fill his lungs again and spoke in a barely audible wheeze. Antonia leaned down to get closer to him, but could only make out every third word. When she tried to get a bit closer to him, the wounded man snapped out a hand to grab her by the throat.

"Fix my leg and get me the hell outta here," he snarled.

"Please . . . don't!"

Bertolucci tried to grab the wounded man's arm, but couldn't get a finger on him before Antonia's face turned beet red and her mouth gaped open for air.

"Take one step closer and I'll squeeze harder," the wounded man threatened.

Bertolucci froze in his tracks. His eyes grew wider as he was forced to watch his assistant struggle to draw her next breath. He only had to watch for another second before a shot cracked through the air and the wounded man's head snapped forward as though it had been kicked by one of the nearby horses.

"Oh my God!" Antonia said as the wounded man's hand fell away from her neck.

Clint walked calmly forward, still holding the smoking Colt in one hand and a dented flask in another. Looking to Antonia, he asked, "You all right?"

"Yes," she replied while touching both hands to her neck and backing away from the broken corpse laying on the ground. "I'll be fine."

"Did he hurt you?"

"Not too badly."

To Bertolucci, Clint said, "I told you two to stay back. When I stopped the buckboard so we could circle back to check on this man, I told you both to follow my lead."

"Yes, you did but—"

"I don't give a damn about any buts," Clint warned. "You hired me to do a job and if you want me to do it, you'll have to accept the fact that I might just know what I'm talking about."

"You're right," Antonia said. "And thank you for being there."

"I was watching the whole time," Clint said. "Sorry that asshole put his hands on you."

"What's that?" Bertolucci asked, eyeing the flask in Clint's hand.

"Just what I said," Clint replied. "Whiskey for cold nights and rainy days."

"Hand it over."

Chapter Twenty-Five

A good portion of the ride into Galveston was made in silence. Bertolucci was a mess of frayed nerves at first, but seemed to relax a bit once he'd had a few drinks from Clint's flask. After a few more drinks, the doctor was slouched over in the back of the buckboard and snoring loudly enough to be heard over the rattling wheels.

Antonia's silence was heavy and troubled. Clint had seen the vaguely haunted look in her eyes before on the faces of others who'd been visited by violence precious few times in their lives. He gave her some time to herself before nudging her and trying to get a smile out of her. With a little bit of patience and some groan-worthy jokes, he was granted with a smirk from the young woman. After that, the mood on the ride improved considerably.

As the sun was dipping below the horizon, the scent of the water was thick in the air. The trial they'd been using ended abruptly at a small cluster of buildings and a short pier. Tied to the pier was a flat boat that was twice as long as it was wide. After bringing the buckboard to a stop between the pier and the largest of the buildings, Clint set the brake and climbed down.

"I'll look for the ferryman," he said.

"You won't find him," Antonia replied. "Not until the morning."

Clint had been so focused on the trail in front of him that he'd barely taken notice of the more obvious things such as the deep purple hue of a sky at dusk. Looking up, he grunted, "Aw hell."

"It's all right," Antonia said as she climbed down as well. "There's always rooms available at the hotel. Wait here and I'll make the arrangements."

Clint took a moment to check on Eclipse. The Darley Arabian was used to long rides, but normally got a chance to stretch his legs with a good, long run. This time, he'd had to walk alongside a buckboard as it was pulled by a team that had a load of iron ore hooked to their backs. The stallion responded well to Clint's attention, but seemed ready to get something to eat and catch a few hours of sleep.

"You and me both, big fella," Clint said.

"What's that?" Bertolucci grunted from the back of the cart.

"We're done for the day," Clint said. "Get up."

"Where?"

"Almost there. We're staying at a hotel by a pier."

"The ferry pier?" Bertolucci asked as he sat up and rubbed his eyes. "Oh, good! We'll be at Pebble Sands tomorrow, bright and early."

"Not too early," Antonia said as she walked out of the hotel. "The ferryman should be here around eleven in the morning and we can't go much farther without him."

"Good," the doctor said while climbing down from the cart. "Sleep does wonders for the body as well as the mind. Did you secure my regular room?"

"I did," Antonia replied.

"Good. I'll see you in the morning." With that, the doctor grabbed the bag with his personal belongings in it and headed into the hotel.

"Seems like he's done this a time or two," Clint mused.

"He comes and goes for supplies quite a bit," she told him. "Carmine also likes to leave the island and wander when he needs inspiration."

"Does this hotel serve a good breakfast?" Clint asked as he hefted his saddlebags onto his shoulder.

"Ham and eggs, usually," she said. "But there's always a lot of it."

"I'm sold."

A quiet settled around them that wasn't at all uncomfortable. Unlike the silence that had come during a good portion of the day's ride, this silence was more tranquil and had a hint of promise that surprised Clint when he felt it. Looking over to Antonia, he allowed his eyes to stay on her for a bit longer than normal.

He'd seen plenty of her recently, but not in the way he saw her now. The smooth skin of her neck sloped upward to become lost in the thick strands of her long hair. When his eyes drifted down along the top of her shoulder, Antonia brushed her hand in that same spot as though she could feel his breath on her.

She pulled in a lungful of air, causing her chest to swell beneath the loose cotton of her blouse. Her nipples were growing erect enough to be seen through the material and she didn't make a move to pull her wrap around her to cover them.

In fact, she stood up straighter as if to display herself to him while looking up in expectation of whatever was to come.

"I'm glad you're here," she said. "How you handled those bandits was . . . impressive."

"Impressive for a gunman?" Clint jibed.

Taking a step closer to him, Antonia whispered, "Impressive for any sort of man."

Clint placed his hands gently upon her hips. She took another step closer, swaying slightly beneath her skirts. She looked up at him with intent and her lips parted with a quiet promise.

She kissed him, quickly and eagerly. When Clint slipped his arms around her waist, she pressed herself tightly against his chest.

Chapter Twenty-Six

In a rush, they were in one of the rooms Antonia had rented for them. Clint didn't know if it was his room or hers. All that mattered was that they were alone in one of those rooms with the door shut while the fires inside of them were still burning. With every second that passed, Clint wanted her more and more. By the time the door to the room shut, he couldn't wait another second to get his hands on her.

She wrapped her arms around him, locking her hands behind his neck so she could look up and kiss him again. When Clint's hands found the small of her back and her rounded backside, she let out a slow, trembling breath.

Clint drew her in close, allowing both hands to settle on her hips and massaging them through the layers of her clothing. Despite the kiss growing in passion and intensity, they both quickly lost interest and started tearing off their clothes one piece at a time. Clint pulled at the various buttons and laces holding her skirts and blouse together, but Antonia had a much easier time stripping him down. Once she had his gunbelt off and his jeans open, she began exploring him with her small hands and probing fingers.

Lingering on his chest, she traced his muscles while closing her eyes and leaning her head back so Clint could kiss her neck and face. Antonia's breathing slowed down and became more deliberate the moment she felt his hands upon her breasts.

When Clint teased her little brown nipples, her eyes snapped open and she smiled widely.

Clint eased her skirts down over her hips, allowing her to step out of them. He then lifted her off her feet and carried her over to the bed which was only a couple strides away. The moment her back was resting on the mattress, Antonia eased her legs open and reached out to pull him closer.

Settling on top of her, Clint stayed still so Antonia could feel every inch of him. Her hands slowly worked their way around his body, moving ever closer to the erection that was growing between his legs. The smile on her face widened when she touched him there. Her fingers wrapped around his rigid cock, stroking him until he was hard as stone.

Unable to wait another second, Clint positioned himself directly between her thighs. Antonia became anxious as well, taking hold of his penis and guiding it to the slick wet lips of her pussy. With a slow push, Clint was inside of her. As he eased in further, Antonia's body became tense and her fingers dug into his shoulders a bit harder.

"You all right?" Clint asked.

"Yes," she whispered. "Don't stop. Just . . . go slow."

Clint propped himself up so he could look down into her eyes, studying her face as he slipped all the way inside of her. After a few easy movements, Antonia was even wetter which allowed Clint to quicken his pace. She squirmed slightly at first, but soon started moaning in pleasure and losing herself in the sensation of having him slide in and out of her damp pussy.

Her body gripped Clint tightly, as if no part of her wanted to let Clint go. She arched her back, pressing her firm breasts against him, breathing deeply as she took him in. As Clint rose up a bit, he pushed all the way inside of her and stayed there until she flicked her eyes open to look at him.

Antonia gripped Clint's arms, locking eyes with him and let out a deep throated groan. When Clint eased out and back in again, she wrapped her legs around him and started clawing at his chest. Clint straightened up and moved her legs apart so he was kneeling between them. Sliding his hands up and down along her inner thighs, he pumped into her with stronger thrusts.

She was completely washed away in the moment by now, responding to his every move. Before long, she reached up with both hands to slide her fingers through her hair while smiling contentedly. Arching her back caused her breasts to move upward and Clint was quick to place his hands on them, massaging vigorously as he continued to thrust his hips.

Her skin was smooth and warm. Her nipples were rigid and sensitive. When Clint moved his hands down along the flat contour of her belly, he watched as her tits bounced and swayed in time to his rhythm. He could feel her breaths becoming quicker and shorter. The contented smile on her face had become more urgent and she instinctually reached down to touch his cock at the spot where it was enveloped by her pussy.

Antonia twitched and writhed when her hand found the nub of sensitive flesh just above her opening. When she took her hand away, Clint put his finger on that very spot so he could rub in small circles as he slid in and out of her.

"Oh God," she whispered. At first, Antonia tried to move his hand to one side. Perhaps she was embarrassed by the almost carnal way she reacted to being touched there or maybe she was just surprised by the intensity of her pleasure. Whatever the reason, she didn't try very hard to discourage Clint from rubbing her.

Clint spent some time just watching and listening to the young woman under him. Her face drifted between serene smiles and passion so intense that she grit her teeth and bit her lower lip until it passed. Soft, subtle moans came from the back of her throat, culminating in breathy gasps as her pleasure reached its peak.

When she climaxed, she grabbed the bed on either side of her and spread her legs open as wide as they could go. Clint could feel her tighten around him until the last tremor of her orgasm faded away. She was wetter than ever now and as Antonia finally collapsed in exhaustion, Clint settled on top of her once again and pumped with a vigorous rhythm.

Antonia opened her eyes again, watching Clint pound into her. She wrapped her arms around him, moaning softly as he entered her. Slowly, she reached down with both hands to spread herself open to invite him to push deeply into her. Clint obliged and drove into her again and again, burying his cock as far into her as it could go before sliding out and back.

Keeping her hands down where they already were, Antonia eased her fingers around Clint's rigid penis. She stroked him as he moved in and out of her like a piston, savoring every inch. Clint reached around with both hands to cup her firm little ass. When he pumped forward, he pulled her close. Antonia responded to that by grabbing Clint in a similar way so she could pull him close as well. Their bodies ground together in a steady rhythm, sweat rolling from their skin as their mouths pressed against the other's in a hungry kiss.

As Clint neared his climax, he could feel Antonia's body tensing for another one of her own. She came in a matter of seconds, her breath catching in her throat as if the explosion inside of her was a complete surprise. Clint didn't last much longer, driving his cock deep inside of her one final time before he was driven over the edge.

Chapter Twenty-Seven

"So," Bertolucci said the next morning, "did you two sleep well?"

The three of them sat around a small circular table. Dawn's faint yellow light came in through a window that had been opened to accept it along with a cool breeze. The scent of hot oatmeal and burnt bacon drifted in from the kitchen and the plates that were spread out on the table, mingling with the smell of hot coffee that had been given to them as soon as the trio had been shown to their seats.

Antonia glanced nervously at Clint, unsure as to what she should say.

It was unclear whether or not Bertolucci was trying to get at something other than the question he'd asked, so Clint said, "I slept great. How about you?"

"Like the proverbial log," the doctor replied. "I barely recall finding my bed last night. Once my head hit the pillow, I was dead to the world. How about you?"

"I slept just fine," Antonia said, and left it at that.

"I was a little restless, at first," Clint commented.

***

Even from the corner of his eye, Clint could tell Antonia was blushing. She tried to cover her face by allowing her hair fall down around it to form a curtain as she silently poked her breakfast with a fork.

"Anxious about getting to the island, I imagine," Bertolucci said.

"I don't know if I was anxious, so much as excited." He looked over to Antonia, who was still trying to stare straight down at her food without reacting.

"There's a lot of exciting times in store," the doctor said eagerly. "That's for certain."

Keeping his eyes on Antonia, Clint said, "I certainly hope so."

She cleared her throat and took a sip of coffee.

"We'll need to see about getting some help loading the cargo onto the boat," the doctor said without taking much notice of his assistant's discomfort. "The faster we get away, the sooner we'll be at Pebble Sands. Once we're there, I can get straight back to work. I must say, Mister Adams, having you there to watch out for my interests is quite a comfort."

"I'm there to watch out for both of your interests," Clint reminded him. "Some more than others."

Finally, Antonia couldn't contain herself. She took a quick kick at Clint's shin under the table, covering the noise with a loud cough.

"Are you sure you're feeling all right, my dear?" Bertolucci asked her.

"I'm fine. I'll feel much better once things get back to normal."

"Normal?" Bertolucci scoffed. "When I'm finished with my innovation, nothing will be normal! People will be travel-

121

ing from one end of this country to the other faster than ever before. Businesses will expand to include entire countries where they only used to serve small towns!"

"And we'll be eating delicacies from exotic lands that we ain't never heard of before," chimed in the portly old woman who'd brought them their breakfast. Smiling warmly, the lady patted Bertolucci's shoulder and said, "You've been talking that way for some time, Doctor. When are those things going to happen?"

"Sooner than you think, Martha," Bertolucci replied. "Especially now that I have—"

"Now that we have plenty of rest," Clint said. When the old woman glanced over at him, Clint rolled his eyes as if they were all simply coddling an imaginative child.

"I see you've heard his speech as well," the woman said.

"I have," Clint told her. "More than once."

"Then just think how many times we've all heard it," she said, twirling her finger around to encompass the entire hotel. "But we still love Doctor Bertolucci just like he was one of our own. Don't we, Harrison?"

In response to that, an old man who'd been huddled over a newspaper at one of the other tables grunted a half-hearted affirmation before turning a page.

The old woman shuffled away, heading for nearby doors leading to the kitchen.

The friendly expression on Clint's face hardened a bit when he said, "You need to stop talking that much, Doc."

"Why?"

"Because we've already been attacked several times. Someone is after you or that cargo you're hauling."

"Probably both," Antonia said.

"Exactly," Clint said. "How is it that she's got a better handle on all of this than you do?"

"I am perfectly aware of what's happening," Bertolucci said somberly. "I've been right there with you during most of these attacks."

"There might not be so many more attacks to come if we all just keep our heads down a bit more. Talking up this big invention of yours to anyone who'll listen isn't helping."

"These good people have heard all of this and plenty more already," Bertolucci said. "Besides, I refuse to live in fear, even if fear is sometimes warranted."

"Being afraid is a damn terrible way to live, I'll grant you that," Clint admitted. "but a little bit of fear is a healthy thing. It's nature's way of letting you know when it's time to protect yourself."

"I am a man of science, Mister Adams. We find ways to bend nature's laws to suit our purposes."

"Yeah," Clint sighed. "So don't tell me you've never gone too far in one direction and been fearful of taking one more step where you might burn yourself to a cinder."

"I consider this place, as well as the island beyond, my home," Bertolucci explained. "If I cower here, then what sort of man am I?"

"Nobody's asking you to cower," Clint said in an exasperated tone. "Just rein it in a bit, huh?"

"I'll try."

"You know what might help?"

Bertolucci's eyes widened. "What?"

"A little bit of good, honest work."

Chapter Twenty-Eight

Clint's last-second idea turned out to be quite the inspiration. First of all, there was only one young man in the vicinity of the hotel who was interested in earning a bit of extra money dragging heavy crates onto a flat boat. Second, Bertolucci was needed to get the crates loaded which kept him busy for a good while. Third, the doctor was so spent afterward that he didn't have enough energy to talk to the ferryman about anything beyond the rate that he would be charged for passage from the mainland to Pebble Sands Island.

Antonia, on the other hand, still had some wind in her sails. "Why wasn't it the same rate as always?" she asked.

The ferryman was a skinny fellow from Louisiana who filled out his coveralls the way a load of potatoes filled a burlap sack. He sat on a small stool near the back of the boat hanging on to the rudder while two slightly smaller men tended to the barge's single sail.

"I gotta charge by the load," the ferryman replied. "This load is pretty damn heavy."

"I'm a regular customer," Bertolucci pointed out.

"And I appreciate that, but this load ain't a regular one. What the hell is in those crates, anyhow?"

As much as he wanted to answer that question, Bertolucci decided against it. The stern glare he saw on Clint's face helped make that decision quite a bit easier.

"I suppose this rate will do," the doctor said.

By the looks of it, the barge had been cobbled together from many different boats. Sections of the body even looked to have come from a stagecoach and been hastily crafted to suit its new purpose. Fortunately, the island wasn't far away.

"So," the ferryman said after a few minutes of quiet, "what're you workin' on now, Doc?"

"Same thing as before," Bertolucci nervously replied.

"That thing with the train tracks?"

"Yes."

"Sounds interesting."

"It is."

The ferryman had yet to look at anyone on the barge for more than a few seconds. At times, he seemed close to falling asleep as he leaned against the rudder to stay on a course that was mostly a straight line. When they arrived at the pier jutting out from the nearby island, he tossed a line to one of his younger helpers and dug a small pipe from his shirt pocket.

"Need any help with unloading?" the ferryman asked as he used a match to light his pipe.

"No," Clint said good-naturedly while grabbing the closest crate. "We brought them this far."

It took some time, but the three of them managed to unload the crates without any help. And since he hadn't been paid for his assistance, the ferryman was more than happy to watch the process while smoking his cheap tobacco.

Chapter Twenty-Nine

Doctor Bertolucci's compound on Pebble Sands Island was fairly impressive. Although small, it was set up to be mostly self-sufficient as far as basic necessities were concerned. There were a few small fields where vegetables and some fruits trees were grown. Fresh water came in through a small stream and a well. There were a couple chicken coops and pens for live-stock. Anything else that was required could be purchased on the mainland or from the ferryman who was more than willing to bring in anything someone might need—for a price.

When the crates were all brought to the largest of the island's four buildings, the only thing Clint needed was somewhere to sit down. Bertolucci had disappeared after carrying a few crates over to the pile Clint had made. Antonia, however, stood on the porch of a house with two floors that looked to have been plucked from New England and dropped onto Texas soil.

"You just going to stand there and watch?" Clint asked.

Antonia smiled and nodded. "Yep."

"I can see why the doctor hired you for his assistant. You're always so helpful."

"I brought some lemonade."

Now Clint smiled. "And," he said as he approached the porch to take the glass she was offering, "you're forgiven."

The lemonade was cool and sweet, but there was something else in the brew that made Clint feel cool on the inside as well. Holding the glass at arm's length, Clint studied it and asked, "What did you put in this?"

"Just a little something the doctor cooked up. Makes water stay cooler for longer."

"Will it make me sick?"

"No."

"Then I don't care what it is," Clint said before downing the rest of the lemonade. "I suppose I should just get used to that while I'm here."

"Cool drinks?"

"No. I mean not knowing exactly what's going on with whatever the doctor is doing."

"Yeah," she said while brushing some of the hair away from her face. "I've been working with him for quite a while and even I don't know everything about everything he's doing."

"Doesn't that make you uncomfortable?" Clint asked.

"I didn't like it at first, but I'm learning. The doctor is actually a very good teacher."

"Yeah, well maybe you can teach me how to be relaxed while handling ore that could blow up in my face."

The crates had all been stacked in the largest of the buildings which was where Bertolucci kept his laboratory. Next to that building was a smaller one that had been built along the shoreline. It resembled a common mill with a set of wheels dipping into the water. As the water moved by, the wheels turned and a mechanism was set into motion. Not a lot could be seen of the mechanism from outside since most of it was connected to and enveloped by the laboratory itself.

Antonia looked over there as she said, "I doubt that ore is really so dangerous."

"It is according to the man who made it."

"Anything can be dangerous in the wrong hands. But, in the hands of someone who knows what they're doing, there's nothing to worry about."

Clint stepped in closer to her. "So you're telling me you like the way I handle dangerous things?"

"I was referring to your pistol, Clint."

"So was I," he said with a wink.

Her cheeks flushed a little, but not nearly as much as when they'd been within earshot of the doctor at breakfast. "Sometimes you need to trust the people who know what they're doing. That goes both ways, you know."

"Yeah," Clint said, his eyes drifting over to the laboratory as well. "And even though the doctor seems more than willing to explain things to me, they don't make a whole lot of sense. Kind of makes me feel like I'm riding a horse with a mind of its own without any reins in my hands."

"I guess that's one way of looking at it."

"So, who is the doctor to you, anyway?" he asked, shifting his gaze back to the young woman in front of him. "You two related?"

"I told you how we met."

"That's right. So there's nothing else going on between you two?"

"Nothing else? Like what?"

Clint didn't say anything, deciding instead to wait the couple of seconds for his meaning to make itself clear to her. In a short amount of time, Antonia was wincing as though she'd been pinched in a tender area.

"Oh!" she exclaimed. "You mean something going on as in . . ." Rather than express the picture that was coming to her mind in words, she scowled and shook her head vigorously. "No, no, no. Not at all. He's never even tried anything inappropriate while we've been together."

"Does he have a wife or lady friend? Maybe some woman he visits back in that little town when he's needing to sow some wild oats?"

"The doctor doesn't have any oats to sow," she chuckled.

"He's a man, Antonia. He may not be like most men, but every one of us has a few things in common. That's one of 'em."

She furrowed her brow and stared into the distance. After some bit of silent pondering, she said, "No. He's never done anything that even came close to inappropriate. At least, not where I'm concerned."

"That's good."

"Why? You jealous?"

"No, but I don't want to get shot at while protecting a man I don't like. And something tells me there's still more shooting to be done."

Chapter Thirty

"Come here, Clint," Bertolucci said. "I want to show you something."

It was early evening and Clint's work was long done. He'd spent a good portion of the rest of his day exploring the island. As far as that was concerned, there wasn't much to see. Pebble Sands was aptly named because, apart from the structures that had been built by man, the main things to see were small rocks and lots of sand.

He'd tried to get Antonia alone, but that didn't go far. After sharing some lemonade with him on the porch, she'd been quick to dive into her work which didn't involve Clint in the slightest.

When he heard those words from the doctor, Clint had been sitting with his feet up on the rail, hands folded on his chest, and eyes pointed toward the water.

"You want to show me something?"

"That's right."

"Like what?"

"What happened to all those questions you were asking?" Bertolucci inquired. "About what I'm doing here and what you're protecting?"

"I gave up on those," Clint replied with a shrug. "Seemed like all I was going to get is a bunch of babble."

Bertolucci waved for Clint to follow him as he started walking slowly toward the laboratory.

"Come on along with me and I'll show you something you can sink your teeth into."

Clint took his feet down from where they'd been propped up on the rail and stepped down from the porch. From there, he was led into the largest building for miles in any direction.

"You want to know what I see?" Bertolucci asked.

"A bunch of wood buildings on a small island?"

"No!" the doctor chuckled. "I mean in regard to the future. What I see is a world made smaller because we can travel from one end of it to the other in a fraction of the time it takes now. And as time goes on, travel will become easier and easier."

"Sure it will. Given enough time, plenty of things will be possible."

"But I'm not talking in centuries or decades," Bertolucci said. "I'm thinking more like a few years."

"What else are you thinking?" Clint asked.

The inside of the large building was completely open. It was one large room the size of three barns. One half of it was filled with tables covered in papers, desks, bookshelves and racks of what looked like surgical instruments. There were other tools as well, many of which Clint didn't recognize. The farthest wall was partly open so it could allow the mechanism from the mill outside to come in. Clint still didn't know exactly what the machine was for, but it was obviously hard at work. Several gauges flickered, needles jumped and gears spun, all in the name of whatever Bertolucci had in mind. He felt as lost and clueless as he had when, several years ago, he had spent some time with Nikola Tesla.

On the other half of the room, running lengthwise down the entire building, were sets of railroad tracks. The tracks were sectioned into portions that looked to be around ten to twenty feet in length and arranged to form a straight line. The breaks in that line were shallow, blackened pits. Each pit was the same size and was also spanned by iron rails that connected the more traditional tracks.

Bertolucci walked to the closest end of the track where a small push cart was waiting. It was a standard model used by railroads to carry a few men and some supplies down the line, powered by a pump operated by a pair of workers. Instead of workers, however, this cart's handles were connected to a machine resembling a large coffee pot. At least, that was the first thing Clint thought of when he saw the large metal cylinder, its conical top and the series of tubes connecting it to the smaller containers connected to the bottom of the larger one.

Clint hadn't even noticed the small switch attached to the side of the kettle-like device until Bertolucci walked over to it and flipped it on.

"This," the doctor said as steam started to rise from the kettle, "represents railroad travel as we know it today."

The pump handles on the cart began to raise and lower thanks to the steaming mechanical device attached to them. As the pump moved, the cart's wheels turned and the little vehicle started to roll.

"It's slow," Bertolucci said. "It's clumsy and it requires a lot of work."

"It's faster than walking or riding," Clint said. "I never found it to be clumsy and plenty of men earn a damn good living doing that work."

The cart had built up a good amount of speed, despite clattering over the joints in the rails where the regular tracks were connected to the sets of iron that bridged the small pits in the ground. When it reached the other end, the cart bumped against a thick wooden barrier fortified by sandbags and posts. Bertolucci ran down to that end and turned off the machine that caused the pump handles to rise and fall.

"Granted, this is just a model," the doctor explained, "but it's more than enough to prove my point. If you'd be so kind as to place a few of those iron strips we acquired into one of the gaps in the middle of my track."

"I've hauled these things from one side of Texas to the other," Clint grunted. "Why not a little farther?"

One of the crates had already been opened before Clint was invited into the laboratory, so he took a strip of ore in each hand and walked it back to the track. Thinking about what the blacksmith had told him, Clint tightened his grip on the iron strips to make absolutely certain they wouldn't slip from his fingers.

After laying the strips in one of the shallow pits beneath the rails going over them, Clint stepped back and said, "Now what?"

"Now," Bertolucci said as he flipped a few more switches on the cart, "step back and witness history in the making."

As before, the device attached to the cart began to steam and the pump handles started to rise and fall. The cart moved in the opposite direction, building up speed just as it had done on its previous journey down the tracks. When it reached the pit containing the ore, the cart lurched forward and sped down the track as though it had been shot from a cannon. Clint barely had enough time to hop away from the tracks before the cart flew past him to slam into the sandbags and posts on that end.

As the dust settled from the cart's stop, Bertolucci stood with his arms outstretched and watching Clint with wild eyes.

Clint almost felt bad for his reaction, but couldn't help asking, "Is that it?"

Chapter Thirty-One

"Is that it?" Bertolucci gasped. "Is that <u>it</u>?"

"Right. Is there any more?"

"Weren't you watching?"

"Yes," Clint replied. "I saw the cart go faster. Is that all this is about?"

"First of all, the cart went upwards of five to six times faster than before. That's an amazing improvement. Second, this is just a model with only one spot where the specially crafted ore was inserted. Just imagine what it will be like with several spots of ore!"

Clint nodded. "I imagine you'd send the cart through a wall. Didn't you say you wanted to use this for passenger trains?"

"Yes, but . . ." Too flustered to finish his sentence, Bertolucci walked over to one of the desks in his laboratory. On it, there were charts of all sizes and ledgers filled with pages of scribbled notes and numbers. "Trains will be speeding across this country with a minimum of work needed to modify the rails. In fact, ninety percent of the tracks that have already been laid can remain."

"What about the trains themselves?" Clint asked. "Won't they fly off the rails?"

"Not once these are installed," Bertolucci said as he pointed to a bundle of what looked to be metal rods that had been flattened and then shaped into curved arc shapes. "These attach to the train wheel covers and secure the locomotive to the tracks."

"What about when they need to switch tracks?"

Bertolucci sighed, sputtered a few random syllables and sighed again. "How do you know so damn much about locomotive design?"

Clint laughed. "I've done some work on the railroads."

"Not everything is perfected yet, obviously," the doctor said as he set down the charts he'd been holding. "That's why I'm here. But trains are just the beginning. My innovation can be outfitted to boats and even smaller wagons for use in cities for public transportation. Those smaller models won't even need to use any fuel whatsoever! They'll be pushed by the ore alone!"

"That sounds interesting."

"Interesting hardly does it justice, but yes. Very interesting, indeed."

Clint gave Bertolucci a few moments to catch his breath before asking, "Is that all?"

"Are you joking?"

Smirking, Clint replied, "All I meant was, is that all you have to tell me? So far, there's been a lot. I'm just trying to find out the whole story since the men coming after you must know it as well."

Bertolucci shrugged his shoulders. "There are plenty of uses for my innovation. I've documented several, but they're not known to anyone but myself."

The more he thought about it, the more Clint saw of the picture Bertolucci was trying to paint. Anything concerning the railroads tended to be big business. Something that had the potential to change the game where the railroads were concerned jumped way past that.

"How close are you to finishing this?" Clint asked.

"Now that I have my ore mostly perfected, I'm very close. Of course, there are still a few drawbacks to using it."

"What sort of drawbacks?"

Bertolucci's eyes drifted from one spot in the lab to another, as if to mimic the thoughts fluttering through his mind. "Some of the technical points you've mentioned. There are design flaws, but those will be ironed out given enough time. There's the ore itself."

"What about it?"

"Well, it needs to be smelted and that's not a cheap process. Then there's maintaining it. I don't honestly know how long it will perform at optimal efficiency."

"What's that mean?" Clint asked.

"It means I'm not even certain if this is the final process to make the ore," Bertolucci said while sweeping a hand to the crates stacked nearby. "Magnets don't typically need much by way of maintenance, but this could be different. Then there's the instability."

"Instability? You mean that ore truly can explode?"

Bertolucci scowled and crossed his arms over his chest. "Ferguson exaggerated that aspect, mostly because he's a perfectionist at heart. That quality makes him an excellent blacksmith, but it also means he tends to err quite greatly on the side of caution."

"I suppose I could see that."

Suddenly, Bertolucci's eyes widened. His mouth hung open and he started looking around as though he barely knew where he was.

"What is it?" Clint asked. "What's wrong?"

"I just thought of something! What if some of the ore treated with my process was used to make gun barrels? All you'd need is a similarly treated bullet and it would leave the barrel at a vastly increased rate!"

"You'd want to use something that could possibly blow up to make gun barrels?" Clint said. "Don't you see anything wrong with that?"

It took a few moments, but Bertolucci eventually nodded. "Perhaps. Perhaps not." He then went to his desk and started furiously working out equations.

Clint left him to it, hoping to God that the doctor didn't find a way to convince himself his new idea had the slightest bit of merit.

Chapter Thirty-Two

Fortunately, Doctor Bertolucci didn't go to work creating a pistol barrel with a better than average chance of blowing up in someone's hand. After a few minutes at his desk, he crumpled up several papers and went back to his track and pump cart. Clint gave himself a tour of the compound by walking nearly every inch of property on Pebble Sands that he could. There was more to the island than Clint had originally thought.

He started by scouting the portions of the island that were used the most. Mainly, Clint looked for places someone could hide or approach the buildings without being noticed. It was next to impossible to keep from being surprised by someone who truly wanted to sneak up on a target, but it never hurt to be prepared.

When it came time to explore the further reaches of the island, Clint put a saddle on Eclipse's back and rode him out of the barn where he'd been kept. After spending so much time on the barge, the Darley Arabian seemed very happy to get in a good run with some solid ground beneath his hooves. There were a few hills covered in trees that concerned Clint since they looked down on the buildings while providing someone a good amount of cover. Knowing where the problem spots were, however, would go a long way in helping Clint if the need arose.

More than anything, the island's size was its biggest asset and its greatest liability. It was a relatively small patch of land which made it easier to protect than some sprawling property that spread out over several acres. If things got really bad, however, there weren't many places to go. Like any other problem, the more he thought about it, the larger it seemed. Clint decided to take what he'd learned, stow it in the back of his mind and get on with his day. No sense fretting about complications that had yet to rear their heads.

Clint found himself on top of one of those hills, not quite the biggest on Pebble Sands but close, looking down at the water. The mainland wasn't far away and as he stood there, he could even see the barge making its way across the water. Perhaps supplies were being brought in to Bertolucci or perhaps the ferryman had another destination in mind.

Eclipse had started grazing nearby, so Clint let the Darley be. He took a canteen from his saddlebag, opened it and splashed some water into his mouth. Squinting into the distance, Clint noticed that the boat he'd spotted wasn't the barge after all. There was no sail on this craft and it seemed to be a bit smaller. There was only room for a few men and maybe a horse or two. Clint put his canteen back into his bag and took out a pair of field glasses he'd found in the compound.

Looking through the lenses, he could see at least two men and two horses on the flat, open boat. The craft was propelled by a small paddlewheel powered by a steam engine that took up most of the back of the boat. It chugged silently, sending a thin plume of smoke into the air, heading straight for Bertolucci's island.

Clint watched for a bit longer until he could make out the face of a man who stood at the front of the boat. That man's eyes were fixed on the island, intent with purpose. Lowering the glasses, Clint climbed back into his saddle and rode down to get a closer look.

Chapter Thirty-Three

The boat came ashore on a short stretch of beach on the opposite side of the island from where Bertolucci had set up his compound. With the island being as small as it was, the cranking of the large machine connected to the laboratory could still be heard. Even so, the landing was made without being seen by Bertolucci or Antonia who were busy working. Clint was working as well, but his job put him in the right place at the right time to watch the small boat make its landing.

The first man to step off the boat was the one who'd made most of the ride while standing at its bow. He was slightly above average height and had a slender build. He walked with confidence that bordered on arrogance as if he was always certain he was being admired from afar. The chiseled cut of his facial features combined with an immaculately trimmed beard looked somewhat aristocratic. The coldness of his squinting eyes gave his appearance an overall cruelty.

The other man who came with him was shorter and younger. He had thick shoulders and arms and walked slightly behind the taller man. His eyes darted back and forth to take in his surroundings and his hand never strayed far from the pistol hanging at his side.

"Stop right there," Clint said from where he stood behind a trio of tall trees. Eclipse was tethered further back where he couldn't be seen, but not too far away.

Both men stopped, their eyes snapping immediately to the spot where Clint was hiding. Although the younger man placed his hand on his pistol and glared at the tree line, the slender man with the well-kept beard put on a smile that didn't even try to seem genuine.

The dapper man held his hands in front of him and raised them slightly. The gesture seemed intended to express an unwillingness to cause trouble as to display the ivory handled .44 holstered on his hip.

Stepping from the cover of the trees, Clint held his Colt in one hand at waist level.

"Who are you?" he asked.

"I'm Anthony Holland," the slender man said in a sharp, European voice. "That's my associate, Wesley."

The younger man gave Clint a fraction of a nod.

"This island is private property," Clint announced.

"I'm aware of that," Holland replied.

"Then what are you doing here?"

"I'm here to have a word with you, Mister Adams."

Clint's eyes narrowed so he could examine the two men even closer. For someone well versed in reading bluffs and tells at a card table, there was plenty to see. The two men in front of Clint weren't about to draw their weapons and blaze away without being provoked, but they would undoubtedly be able to defend themselves. As far as whether or not they were going to attack Clint a little later, that remained to be seen.

"Have we met before?" Clint asked.

To Clint's surprise, it was Wesley who replied, "We have."

"You don't look familiar," Clint admitted.

"That's because it was just over a card game in Wyoming."

"Perhaps you two can get reacquainted," Holland offered. "I'd like to offer you a drink while we talk. Perhaps afterward, we can sit down to a game or two."

"Sounds real sociable, but I'll have to refuse. Mostly because you won't be here long enough for all of that."

"Is that any way to treat guests?"

"You weren't invited here," Clint said. "Also, I have a feeling you're not here to socialize."

"Really? Then what am I here for?" Holland sneered.

"I don't know," Clint replied. "But, whatever it is, I wish you'd get on with it and be on your way."

Holland stared at Clint with a cool, calculating stare. Angling his head to one side, he raised a finger and said, "Actually, I'd like to show you something. Wesley . . ."

When the younger man started to move, Clint put his hand on his Colt. "I'd advise you think real careful about what move you plan on making," he warned.

Wesley's lip curled back in a tense snarl. Every muscle in his body wanted to respond to Clint's threatening stance but was being held in check by the man closest to him.

"Easy," Holland said. "I assure you, Mister Adams, my associate is merely getting something from our boat to show you our intentions."

"Yeah," Clint growled. "I'll just bet he is."

"Why are you so aggressive?" Holland inquired. "Is this how Doctor Bertolucci asked you to greet trespassers?"

"No, it's how I treat men when they try to sneak up on me in the dead of night."

145

"We came here at night, but we hardly snuck."

"That's splitting hairs. If you'd wanted to have a civil word with the doctor, you would've come to the pier. Better yet, you would've announced yourself ahead of time."

"True, but I didn't want to speak to the doctor," Holland countered. "I want to speak with you. Now, will you allow Wesley to retrieve my item or should we just leave without you ever knowing why we came here at all?"

Clint knew better than to let curiosity get the better of him. However, allowing Holland to think he was manipulating Clint in some way might get him to relax and tip his hand at some point. Since Holland seemed intent on talking, Clint decided to let him talk.

"All right," Clint said. "But if you or your friend there makes one move I don't like, I'll burn you down."

"Of course," Holland said through a toothy smile.

Chapter Thirty-Four

Like a well-trained dog, Wesley went to the boat and took out a small box in slow, timid movements. Even though he obviously wanted to snap free of his leash and sink his teeth into his prey, Wesley carried the box to the shore and set it down.

"What's that?" Clint asked.

Holland nodded to Wesley, which was the signal for the box to be opened so it contents could be displayed. Wesley held a small brick in his hand. It was about the size of a bible and a deep black color that had a slick, greasy sheen.

"Look familiar?" Holland asked.

"Is that the doctor's ore?" Clint said.

"It was made by a similar process, but not from his personal supply."

"You got it from the blacksmith."

"Your doctor friend isn't the only one who can hire his services."

"And you want me to get more for you," Clint sighed. "If that's it, the both of you can just get back into that little boat and sail back to the mainland."

"There's more, Mister Adams. Much more." With that, Holland opened his jacket to reveal the trim lines of his vest. Being careful to move slowly, he reached for the inner pocket of his jacket and eased something from it.

Clint tensed, preparing to take a shot. He'd even picked his first two targets when he realized Holland wasn't drawing a weapon after all. At least, it wasn't a weapon of the modern day. It was a hammer. Small and pointed at one end, the hammer had a polished head that glinted in the small bit of light coming down from the moon and stars.

Holland held it so Clint could get a good look at the mallet before he took it over to where Wesley was standing. Once again, Clint tensed. The only thing Wesley did was grab the oily brick by one corner and remove a piece of it from the whole. Now, Clint could see the brick had actually been four separate pieces in the first place. One of those pieces was placed on top of a rock protruding from the ground and the rest were put back into the box Wesley had gotten from the boat.

Squatting down like a child trying to examine a bug, Holland tightened his grip on his mallet, raised it high above the section of brick and brought it down with a sharp crack. Sparks flew from the spot where mallet met the ore, some of which crackled brightly in the air above the rock.

Holland stood up and quickly backed away.

The sparkling crackles continued over the ore, snapping like fireworks on a summer night. The crackling grew louder and faster until the ore itself appeared to be emitting them on its own. A second later, there was a powerful thump and the ore blew apart in an explosion of smoke and ash.

Clint, Holland and Wesley were knocked back by a shockwave that pulsed from the explosion in a single blast. Although the blast took Clint off his feet, the sound it made was muffled and quieter than a gunshot. Clint's ears were ringing, but only from the impact of the blast rather than any sound it made. When he climbed back to his feet, he still felt the sensation of being knocked down by a ghost.

"What the hell was that?" Clint asked.

"That," Holland replied, "was the sound of a fortune waiting to be made. Believe it or not, the ore that created that explosion was the same as the one Doctor Bertolucci had you transport to this island."

After what he'd been told by the blacksmith who'd helped create the ore, Clint had no trouble believing it.

In his mind, Clint ran through every single time one of those crates had been jostled during the ride or on the train. He thought about every time a crate was set down with just a bit too much force. More than once, he could recall times when the cart had run over a hole in the road that might have caused an impact rivaling the one from Holland's mallet. "What did you do to set it off?" he asked.

"Just what you saw," Holland said. He flipped the mallet in his hand, savoring every moment. "That ore has more uses than you've been told, Adams. Sure, it can be made to help push a train a little faster or propel some wagons along a specially made track within the confines of a city. But what you've seen here," he added while motioning to the smoldering pit where the corner of the brick had been, "is a whole other story."

"Why show this to me?"

"Because you can help me take full advantage of Bertolucci's creation. What he wants to do is child's play. It's like using a cotton gin as a music box."

"Or a rifle as a club," Clint said dryly.

"If that's how you'd like to see it."

"From the way you're talking, that's the only way to see it. You're not the first man to come along who wants to turn a useful tool into a weapon. Dynamite was intended to help mining and construction until someone decided to light a fuse and toss it into a group of men."

"That's the way humanity works, Mister Adams," Holland said. "We are violent and bloodthirsty. We are also inventive and creative. Besides, who said I wanted to use this invention to harm anyone? You just saw an explosion and decided to jump to conclusions."

"Did I?" Clint scoffed. "Then pardon the hell out of me. I guess I'll just take myself and my primitive thoughts away from your glorious presence."

Holland allowed Clint to walk all of five feet away from him before saying, "Hold it."

Clint stopped but didn't turn around. Every one of his senses were so attuned to the two men behind him that he would have heard the scrape of a finger against leather if one of them tried to draw on him. More than that, it simply didn't make sense for Holland or his hired gun to shoot him. Not yet, anyway.

"I'm listening," Clint said.

After a few quiet moments, Clint turned back around. As he'd figured, neither man had moved from their previous spot.

"All I want is a larger sample of Bertolucci's ore," Holland said. "And a copy of his research notes."

"A copy?"

"The originals would do nicely," Holland said. "I just figured it might be easier for you to scribble down a few things. I can give you some pointers if you'd want to know what sort of thing I'm looking for."

"Oh, would you? How kind. How about I think about it?"

Holland seemed genuinely surprised to hear those words. "I can pay handsomely, I assure you."

"While I'm thinking, I don't want you to step foot on this island again and don't even think about approaching the doctor or his assistant."

"Done."

It was the best Clint could hope for at that moment. Even so, he stayed nearby to watch the two men climb into their boat and sail away.

Chapter Thirty-Five

Clint wanted to approach Bertolucci right away with what had happened. It was late, though, and then decided to wait until morning. On his way back to the main house where they all had their own bedrooms, Clint saw a light still burning inside the large laboratory building.

He approached a window, thinking Bertolucci may have left a lantern burning or possibly even fallen asleep in front of one of his experiments. What he saw instead was the doctor sitting at his desk, scribbling away in one of his journals. For some reason, that ruffled Clint's feathers enough for him to push open the door and march inside.

"Have you been here the whole time?" Clint asked.

Bertolucci didn't even look up from his journal.

"Hey!" Clint shouted.

The doctor snapped his head up and looked around, glancing upward at first as if he truly thought the voice might have come from that direction instead of one of the lab's doors. "Oh," he said sleepily. "It's you."

"Right, it's me. When the hell were you going to tell me?"

"Tell you what?"

"That the ore we were transporting was explosive!"

Bertolucci ran his hands flat against the top of his head, slicking back his hair while letting out a tired groan.

"Haven't we already gone through this? Ferguson was being overly cautious. The ore is fine as long as it's handled properly."

"Properly, huh? And what if there's too big of a bump? What if something heavy falls onto a piece of it? Or what if one of those carts scrapes it the wrong way?"

"Whatever are you talking about?"

Frustrated beyond words, Clint walked over to a pile of scrap pieces of ore near one end of the tracks running the length of the lab. Finding a chunk that was just over half as big as the piece that Holland had used, Clint set it in the middle of an open space and then stomped over to one of the many workbenches.

"Clint, it's late," the doctor said. "There's a lot I need to do. Can't this wait until morning, when I've gotten some sleep? Or afternoon, perhaps?"

Clint found what he was after with just a bit of searching. The mallet was slightly larger than the one Holland had used, which suited him just fine. Gripping the mallet in one hand, Clint marched over to the small chunk of ore and lifted his hammer high above his head.

"Got anything to say?" Clint asked, watching Bertolucci intently.

The doctor squinted at him, rubbed his eyes and squinted some more. "Is that a hammer you've got?"

"Yep."

"Why?"

Clint picked up the piece of ore with his other hand to show it to the doctor. When Bertolucci merely blinked quizzi-

153

cally at him, Clint dropped the ore and brought the mallet up again. Surely an idiot could piece together Clint's intentions by now. Bertolucci would make the connection any moment.

After several moments, the doctor was still staring blankly at him.

Clint brought the mallet down onto the piece of ore. It struck the rock with a sharp cracking sound, breaking many small chunks off of every one of its edges. Clint stepped back in a quick series of steps, his eyes locked on Bertolucci in anticipation of the panic that would surely appear on the doctor's weary face.

The panic never came.

Neither did the explosion.

"Are you through?" Bertolucci asked.

Clint walked over to the desk where the doctor sat and struck it with the mallet hard enough to bury the head of the tool into the polished wood.

"We are definitely not through with this," Clint said as he turned and headed for the door. "Not by a mile!"

Chapter Thirty-Six

Breakfast was a quiet affair.

It was late in the morning when Doctor Bertolucci stumbled out of his bedroom and made his way down the narrow stairs inside the two story house built in the middle of the island compound. Antonia had been up earlier and made coffee with griddle cakes and some bacon. Clint had been up even earlier than both of them, eating some of the cakes when they'd been fresh out of the pan and opting to have his coffee on the porch.

He heard movement inside the house and bided his time before opening the door and looking straight back through the front parlor into the dining room. Bertolucci was getting up from his seat, tugging at the napkin that he'd tucked into his collar to catch the syrup that would have spilled onto his shirt.

"There you are," Bertolucci said.

"You done eating?" Clint asked.

"Yes."

"Then why don't you step outside so we can have a word?"

The doctor looked nervously at Antonia, who merely looked away before busying herself by cleaning off the dirty dishes. Seeing he wasn't getting any help from his assistant, Bertolucci walked slowly to the front door.

When Clint reached behind the doctor to make sure the door was shut behind him, Bertolucci flinched and threw his hands up to protect his face.

"What are you so fidgety about?" Clint asked.

"You…asked me to come outside. Isn't that customarily how fistfights are arranged?"

"Sometimes. Can you think of any reason why I might want to punch you?"

The doctor's response was as timid as it was uncertain. "Umm . . .no? Although you did seem rather upset last night."

"Yes, which is why I thought I'd wait until we'd all had some rest before I talked to you about what happened."

"Something happened?"

Clint crossed his arms and scowled down at the doctor. "You're a smart man, Carmine."

"All right, fine. You obviously somehow learned about detonating the ore."

"You didn't hear the explosion?"

"No! But that's part of the intriguing aspects in that regard," Bertolucci said. "Did Antonia tell you something about that?"

"No. Anthony Holland came to the island after dark."

That caused some of the color to drain from Bertolucci's face. "He did?"

"He showed me a chunk of that stuff explode right in front of me."

"Wait. How did he get his hands on some of my ore? I checked it before I went to bed and as soon as I awoke. None of it was missing!"

"From your supply, maybe," Clint said. "He's getting his hands on it from somewhere else."

"That damn blacksmith," Bertolucci grumbled.

"That doesn't matter," Clint quickly said. "Anyone with money to spend and a will to get something is gonna get it. What I don't like is that you've been playing down how dangerous this ore of yours is. Just a small nugget of it blew a damn pit into the ground and knocked grown men off their feet! You're telling me it's not dangerous?"

"It takes a very specific chain of events to set off that ore. You couldn't get it to do anything dangerous, could you?"

"No. Tell me why."

"First, you tell me what Holland said to you when—"

Clint cut that sentence short by reaching out to grab hold of the front of Bertolucci's shirt. Pulling him closer and lifting the doctor onto his tip-toes, Clint glared straight into the other man's eyes and said, "You know why I took this job?"

Bertolucci attempted to respond, but could only make a few sputtering noises.

"I took it because you were in real danger and because men like you can be a real danger."

"M-men like me?"

"That's right. Men who tinker with dangerous things without taking the time to think it all through. You see, if men are after you and want to even kill you, that means you've got something valuable to them. You're not carrying money or anything as straightforward and valuable as gold, so that must have been something different. What you were carrying seemed even worse because killers want it so damn badly."

"I told you what it was. I told you what I wanted to do."

"And you seemed honest enough. Maybe not completely honest, but honest *enough*. I gave you the benefit of the doubt, partly because I was curious and partly because there seemed to be something lurking just out of what I could see and I don't much care for that."

Clint eased up on the doctor just enough to allow the smaller men to stand on his own feet. He let go of Bertolucci's shirt, but held him in place with an unwavering stare.

"You told me you'd let me know more about what's going on," Clint said. "You promised to fill in the gaps of what you'd already explained when the time was right."

"Did I?"

"I don't hold it against you that other men were shooting at me. I expected as much when I agreed to work for you. But when I see rocks charged up through some process I don't even understand so they can push a train or blow up when hit with a hammer, that opens a whole other can of worms. Do you have any idea how much damage that ore can do if it fell into the wrong hands?"

"That's why I'm working in secret," Bertolucci insisted. "That's why I asked you to keep this island safe."

"And why didn't you just tell me everything right at the start?"

"Because there was no way of me knowing if you would betray my trust or not. For all I knew, you could take what I told you and gone to Mister Holland or McPike."

"What about after I already proved myself by getting shot at and saving your life?" Clint asked.

"We weren't in a safe place," Bertolucci said. "There were people around who could have heard."

"We've been on this island for a while now."

"Yes and as soon as I got here, I threw myself back into my work. Everything else has been pushed aside. Everything. I'm sorry about that."

All Clint had to do was look at the stubble on Bertolucci's face and the bags under his eyes to know that was true. "If you want to push this aside any longer," Clint warned, "I'm through here."

"I don't want that. Heaven knows you've earned that much."

Chapter Thirty-Seven

While some men might have felt safer in a church or in their home, Bertolucci had his laboratory. In many respects it was his version of a church. It was where he felt safe. It was where he witnessed his wonders. It was his sanctuary. Therefore, it was no big surprise that he wanted to take Clint there to have their talk.

Sitting at one of the smaller desks in the place, Bertolucci reached into one of its drawers and removed a bottle of wine. He looked at the label for a few seconds, letting the constant churn of the machinery being powered by the water outside to calm his nerves.

"Care for a drink?" the doctor asked.

Clint pulled up a stool and sat down near the desk. "Sure," he said.

Bertolucci poured some wine into two dented tin cups and handed one of them to Clint. He took a sip and nodded in appreciation of the vintage. Clint took a drink as well. It was strong stuff for wine, but very flavorful.

"I never intended my ore to have its explosive properties," Bertolucci said.

"I guessed as much."

"When I discovered it, the sequence of events seemed so random. So particular. I honestly didn't think I needed to worry about replicating it again. But, on the off chance that I might be in danger later during my studies, I took notes of what happened in my journal. Never can be too careful, right?"

Clint smirked and took another drink.

"It was a combination of silver and a somewhat rare mineral that set it off," the doctor explained.

Clint thought about asking what the mineral was, but decided against it. He'd worked with plenty of iron and handled his fair share of gold, but was no expert on minerals beyond that. Better to just let the doctor talk at his own rate while he was in a talkative mood.

"I was trying to make the ore myself, you see," Bertolucci told him. "I thought wearing it down with various other materials might help. Anyway, let's just say that when I used that particular combination, I was quite surprised."

Even though the doctor chuckled at the memory, he needed some more wine to help wash it away.

"One of my previous lab assistants barely escaped injury. He decided to part ways with me and I figured he was simply frightened by the affair. As it turned out, he went to someone he knew who worked with certain industrialists in an attempt to sell them information."

"That man was Anthony Holland?"

"No, but he worked with Holland and he hired someone to kill my former assistant so he wouldn't tell what he knew to anyone else. That's where McPike comes into this story."

"I sure didn't take McPike for an industrialist," Clint joked.

"Truth be told, I don't even know for certain who hired McPike in the first place, but I do have some suspicions. That one's been content to let his gun hand do the work while he sits in some fancy office back east."

"East?"

"Boston, most likely," Bertolucci said. "That's where my assistant ran to when he left me. He could have gone somewhere else, I suppose."

"It's probably Boston," Clint said. "I've known plenty of assholes from Boston."

Both men laughed at that before Bertolucci stared down at his desk. "He met with me once, probably in the same fashion that he met with you. Holland asked me to work with him. For him, actually. When I refused, he offered to buy my journals. If this is my cathedral," he said while looking around at the lab surrounding him, "than those journals are my bible. That probably sounds silly to you."

"Not at all," Clint replied. "A man's life work is his religion in a way. It's what he lives by and lives for."

"You understand. But to see my life's work turned into something horrible . . . that's quite unsettling."

"I'm a gunsmith," Clint told him. "I understand that as well."

"So did Holland make that offer to you?"

"Yes."

"And?"

"I refused," Clint said.

But Bertolucci didn't seem to take much solace from that. Considering his history with other assistants, Clint couldn't exactly blame him.

"I try not to think about the terrible ways my inventions can be used. If I thought too much about that sort of thing, I couldn't go on. I suppose part of me was hoping that if I kept pretending hard enough that things weren't so bad, others would believe it too."

"You can't let it stop your work," Clint said reluctantly. "Seems like there's some real possibilities with what you're doing. Is there any way to keep that ore from exploding? Maybe adding something different into the mix?"

"It's not that simple," Bertolucci sighed. "I was lucky to get the ore to work once. Starting again from scratch could take another lifetime. Or two."

"Well, if it's just a magnet . . ."

"It's not just a magnet!" the doctor roared as he swept everything off the top of his desk with one sweep of his hand. He immediately got up to pick things up off the floor, speaking in a more controlled voice.

"That's a simple way of putting it, but there's a lot more to it. Simple magnets couldn't move something as large as a train. They also couldn't provide power to it and the stations along the way."

Clint was stooping down to pick up a few fallen papers as well when he asked, "What do you mean by powering the stations?"

"Have you ever seen experiments with electricity?"

"Yes. I was involved with Nikola Tesla for a short time."

"Indeed?" The doctor seemed very interested. "You will have to tell me about that some time."

"I know I've heard a few things about electrical lights and such. We can talk about Tesla another time."

"Very well. It could start by powering lights and then powering water pumps and mills on the days when there's not enough wind or water current to turn a paddle."

Suddenly, Clint looked over to the machine that took up one side of the laboratory. "Is that what that thing is?" he asked while pointing to the giant mechanism.

"It generates the power I need to conduct my experiments," Bertolucci explained. "Using wind and water and when that's not enough, yes, the ore. Even if there's no breeze and the water dries up, those gears will keep turning."

"Impressive."

"I thought so." Bertolucci watched the machine do its work before saying, "That explosion was a mistake. I tried to put it behind me, but the first thing Holland did was figure out a way to replicate it even easier. You see, he had a mallet made from the mineral that reacts to my ore and coated it with silver to provide the spark. It made me ashamed to be a scientist. After seeing how many men lined up to acquire a new way to kill more people with minimum effort, it made me ashamed to be human."

Chapter Thirty-Eight

That day was one of those that taught a man the difference between peace and quiet. It was quiet, to be certain. The air rustled across the top of the water, carrying the gulf's spray to the compound where Bertolucci conducted his research. Clint remained outside, walking the compound and visiting the different lookout spots he'd scouted earlier.

The skies were gray, giving the water a thick, ominous appearance. Clint spotted a few boats in the distance and even caught sight of the ferry that had brought him to Pebble Sands in the first place. None of those craft came close to the doctor's island, which didn't do anything to help ease Clint's state of mind.

His rifle was kept on hand at all times, along with his field glasses. Clint examined every stray sound he heard and every hint of movement he saw. His muscles were always ready to bring the rifle to his shoulder, but a target had yet to present itself.

There were a few false alarms here and there. A rustle in some trees turned out to be a small animal. A few boats on the water steered toward the island for a short time, but eventually turned to the west or east. Clint watched every one of those with the same amount of readiness. After the visitors he'd gotten already on the island and the train beforehand, he wasn't about to let his guard down for any reason.

And yet, despite all of his preparations and diligence, Clint knew all too well that he could never be in two places at once. Only if he could pull off a feat like that could he protect an island on all sides. That didn't mean he was going to stop trying, though.

The doctor stayed busy in his lab. Ever since confiding everything to Clint, he worked with even more passion. He rarely stuck his nose out of his laboratory. When he needed to eat or drink, Antonia got him what he needed. Every time she stepped outside, she looked for Clint. On those occasions when he was in the area, she met his gaze and smiled.

Clint would nod or tip his hat, but he was too intent on doing his job to smile. That's how it was for that entire day. That's how it was for the next two days after it. Clint, Antonia and Bertolucci would meet for breakfast and supper, sharing a few bites of food and some lemonade or coffee. After the meal was done, the three of them went back to their self-appointed spots.

For those days, even though Clint was constantly ready for it, danger didn't come.

Even when there was nothing to see, he didn't stop looking.

His muscles felt worn just from being so ready.

Quiet days, indeed, but far from peaceful.

Chapter Thirty-Nine

It was after supper when Antonia approached Clint carrying two cups of hot coffee in her hands. He was on the porch of the house, rifle propped against the wall behind him and eyes gazing out at the darkness surrounding the compound. The water churned in the blackness, making it sound as though something was always crawling toward the island.

Antonia came out to stand beside him, set one cup on the railing and rested that hand on his shoulder. Feeling him twitch, she asked, "When was the last time you slept?"

"Last night," he replied.

"No, I mean really slept. When was the last time you slept like a log and woke up feeling as fresh as the new day?"

Clint smirked and took the coffee that had been placed near his hand. "That's quite a poetic way to put it. Can't say as I remember ever sleeping that well."

"What about somewhere close to that?"

"It's been a while for that, too."

"I can tell," Antonia said. "You look like you're wound pretty tight."

"Aren't we all?"

"The doctor always has himself worked into a lather about something," she sighed. "And if he's not worried about some formula or other, he's excited about some breakthrough that's just out of his reach. Either way, it makes for some long days."

"What about you?" Clint asked. "Do you just do your work and go to sleep like a baby every night?"

"No, but that's why I thought I'd have this little talk with you."

Bringing the cup to his nose, Clint sniffed it and asked, "Did you put some whiskey in this? Maybe some kind of tonic that'll knock me on my ass for a few days?"

"No, but that may not be a bad idea." Antonia leaned against the railing next to Clint, holding her coffee so the steam from her cup drifted up into her face. "I think I may have a better idea to help relax you, though."

"I may be coming up with one or two ideas myself."

Antonia reached out to place her hand on Clint's face while leaning in to kiss him on the lips. Their mouths barely drifted an inch apart before she kissed him again. This time, her lips parted so she could flick her tongue on his mouth before nibbling on his lower lip. Clint snaked an arm around her waist, pulling her tight against him so he could feel the soft touch of her breasts pressing against his chest. He kissed her on the lips first before working his way over to her neck.

"That's about what I was thinking," he whispered before nibbling her earlobe.

"Is that all you were thinking?" Antonia asked.

"Not even close."

Chapter Forty

In the middle of the day, the quietest place within the compound was the main house. Bertolucci would be locked in his lab for hours before he even thought about taking a step outside and normally Clint and Antonia would be gone as well. This time however, the two of them were in the cozy room Antonia called her own.

After sneaking up there like a couple of overaged kids with hot blood running through their veins, they began peeling the clothes off of each other. As soon as they were both down to what God gave them, Antonia knelt in front of Clint and placed her hands on him. Slowly, she slid her palms along his hips and stomach as her lips wrapped around his stiffening cock.

Clint let out a long breath when he felt her take every inch of him past her lips. Her tongue moved against him while her head bobbed back and forth. Antonia reached up while sucking him so she could scrape her fingernails down along his chest. Soon, she allowed him to slip from her mouth and looked up at him.

Helping her stand up again, Clint asked, "Is this how you help the good doctor relax as well?"

Her eyes widened and her face twisted into a shocked expression. Slapping both hands against his chest, she shoved him backward until Clint's legs knocked against the side of her bed. He flopped down onto the mattress and she shook her head while climbing on top of him.

"You'd better apologize for that," she said.

Clint merely grinned up at her while gripping her hips in both hands.

Keeping herself poised above him so just the slightest bit of him touched the wet lips between her legs, Antonia said, "Say you're sorry."

Clint held out for all of two more seconds before letting out a frustrated breath and apologizing profusely.

"That's better," she whispered while easing herself the rest of the way down.

Clint let out a slow breath as well, savoring every second as Antonia's slick pussy slid all the way down to the base of his shaft. Once there, she started rocking back and forth, placing her hands on his chest and closing her eyes.

Antonia's body was soft and warm to the touch. As she rode him, her hair spilled down over her shoulders to cover her pert breasts in a silky wave. Her hair was long enough for it to drift across Clint's skin. When he hit a particularly sensitive spot inside her, she arched her back so her hard little nipples protruded from the curtain of hair that had been covering them.

Clint looked up at her, sliding both hands up along the curves of her hips and sides. When he got to her breasts, Antonia sighed gratefully and clasped her hands over his so they wouldn't move away. Clint massaged her ample curves, teasing her nipples until she started to tremble with pleasure.

The moment Antonia stopped moving on top of him, Clint started moving beneath her. He started by grinding his hips and eventually began pumping up between her legs. Antonia responded out of animal instinct, once again bracing her hands on his chest while getting her legs beneath her so she could squat on top of him. That way, when Clint thrust upward, she could move down. When he pulled back, she rose up. When their bodies met, it was with a hard, pounding rhythm.

Every time he impaled her, Antonia let out a breathy grunt. Her nails dug deep into his chest. When her head lolled forward so she could look down into his eyes, her hair fell around both of their faces to block out everything else around them.

Clint reached up to wrap one arm around Antonia to pull her down on top of him. With his other hand, he reached down to grab hold of her buttocks and keep her tight against him. Holding her in place, he began pumping into her with powerful thrusts. Sweat dripped from both of their bodies as Antonia clawed at the mattress on either side of Clint while he continued to drive into her with building momentum.

Suddenly, Antonia let out a series of quick breaths. Clint could tell by the way her entire body tensed that she was in the middle of a powerful climax. He drove all the way into her one last time and stayed there until she could catch her breath.

Antonia sat up, sweeping her hair behind her ears so she could see what Clint was doing. He'd gotten out from beneath her and knelt at one end of the bed. Without a word, he turned her around and bent her over. Knowing exactly what he had in mind, Antonia opened her legs for him and stretched out with both arms while lifting her rounded backside up.

Her back made a sloping curve and Clint ran his hands along her hips while settling behind her. He was so hard and she was so wet that it took hardly any effort at all for him to enter her one more time. From behind her, Clint could drive even deeper than before. He grabbed her hips, pulling her close every time he pounded between her wet thighs.

"Yes," she groaned through her straining breaths. "Fuck me."

Clint smiled when he heard those words coming out of her mouth. Keeping one hand on her backside, he reached forward to take hold of her long hair. "You like that?" he asked while pulling just hard enough to force her head back a little.

"Oh god, yes."

Clint pulled her hair just enough to take out the slack, holding her head in place while he pounded into her. Arching her back, Antonia began to shudder as another orgasm started to work its way through her body.

When Clint let go of her hair, Antonia's head drooped down as if she didn't have the strength to hold it up. He put his hands on her shoulders and filled her with every inch of his rigid cock.

"Give it to me," she moaned. "Give it all to me."

Clint shifted his hands back to her hips and took hold of her. Fully giving herself to him, Antonia rested her head and chest on the mattress while propping her ass up as much as she could. When Clint slid into her from that angle, she climaxed almost immediately.

Antonia's body tensed and she let out a full-throated scream. If she hadn't also pushed her face into a pillow, she would have been heard all the way back on the mainland.

Clint took hold of her rounded backside and pumped into her until he felt the pleasure inside him reach its peak. With one more thrust, he emptied himself into her while letting out a deep groan.

Completely spent, both of them collapsed onto the bed.

"There now," Antonia gasped. "You feel more relaxed?"

"Yeah," Clint replied. "Whether or not I'll be able to move again is something else entirely."

Chapter Forty-One

"Clint!"

That single word, shouted on an otherwise quiet day, hit Clint's ears like a left hook. It was the day following Antonia's miracle cure and Clint had indeed been feeling more relaxed. His patrols continued and he was still vigilant, but his senses seemed sharper. There simply wasn't anything to sense. At least, not until he heard Doctor Bertolucci scream his name.

Clint was in the saddle riding along a small strip of beach when Bertolucci's voice reached him. Snapping the reins, Clint got Eclipse moving toward the compound which was just over a small rise. Before cresting the rise, he already had his rifle drawn from its boot and was looking for something to kill.

Bertolucci stood near the building where his laboratory was built. Waving his arms and jumping up and down, the doctor shouted for Clint even after he'd spotted the Darley Arabian stallion galloping straight toward him.

"Clint!"

"What?" Clint shouted while swinging down from his saddle. Eclipse hadn't even come to a full stop before Clint's boots hit the dirt. "What is it? What's wrong?"

"Come here!" Bertolucci said. "Come quickly!"

"Wait!"

But the doctor had already turned around and was racing back behind the laboratory. Clint followed him, intending on catching up to the older man but inexplicably failing to do so.

Bertolucci may have been older, but he was too worked up to slow down. The only way Clint caught him was because the doctor came to an abrupt stop once he reached the small lot in back of his lab.

"Look," Bertolucci said. "Isn't it beautiful?"

Behind the laboratory, in a spot that had been just a clear plot of land, was a series of tracks laid out in a long oval shape. There was even a series of inclines ranging from a bump in the ground to a small hill. All in all, there was nearly enough track to encircle the entire building.

"When on earth did you do all of this?" Clint gasped.

"I've been working on it for days! With all of the riding around you've been doing, haven't you noticed?"

"I guess I've been more interested in what's going on around this place than in it."

"Haven't we come to something of an understanding?" Bertolucci asked. "I'm more than willing to explain . . ."

"No more explanations," Clint said. "Maybe it's best if we just stick to what we're best at."

Bertolucci smiled. "You don't want explanations? How about a demonstration?"

"Like the one with the pump car?"

"No. This is something much more interesting. See for yourself." With that, Bertolucci swept an arm toward the tracks where a small train rested in the middle of a straight section of track. The engine was simple, resembling an iron coffin with a smoke stack. There were two cars attached to it, each of them plain wooden boxes on wheels. Clint couldn't figure exactly, but the size of the train seemed somewhere in the vicinity of a quarter the size of a real train car. Probably a little smaller.

Bertolucci went to the engine, reached inside through a small round hole and threw a switch that caused a mechanism inside to rattle. Smoke soon drifted up from the stack and the pistons began to move. Before long, the model train was ambling down the tracks.

"There's just enough fuel inside to keep it going less than halfway around," Bertolucci explained. "See that spot there?"

After looking at almost every other spot he could see to make sure there wasn't a threat in the area, Clint looked at the place where Bertolucci was pointing. It was a section of track just around a bend in the tracks where a shallow rut had been dug beneath the iron rails. Like the ones inside the lab, the rut was filled with a narrow bundle covered in what looked to be burlap.

"Is that some of the ore under there?" Clint asked.

"Very observant. Now watch!"

The cart reached the spot a few seconds later. When it rolled over the burlap bundle, the engine lurched forward and picked up a good amount of speed. Along with that, the cars attached to it glowed with a harsh white light coming from several glass tubes attached to their sides. The tubes were almost as big as whiskey bottles and were held in place by brass brackets.

"Damn!" Clint said. "Is all that just because of the ore?"

"It is! It is, indeed," Bertolucci replied excitedly. "Do you see the sparks?"

Those sparks were hard to miss, since they shot out of the engine and attached cars on both sides.

"Yeah," Clint said. "Is that supposed to happen?"

"That's excess energy produced by the components within the locomotive's structure," Bertolucci explained. "It could be used to power other devices within the cars, more lights, or any number of things!"

The engine slowed a bit, but was still moving along pretty well when it reached the next spot in the tracks covering a burlap bundle. Upon crossing that spot, the engine got another jolt of speed and the lights burned even brighter.

"Can the energy be stored somewhere?" Clint asked.

For the first time since the engine had started to move, Bertolucci took his eyes off of the little train. Staring at Clint with genuine admiration, he said, "What an excellent question."

Clint couldn't help but smirk and shrug his shoulders like a boy who'd been praised for correctly adding figures written on a chalkboard.

Bertolucci looked back to the train as it successfully climbed the smaller of three slopes built under the tracks.

"I'm working on a kind of fuel cell to store the energy. Once that's complete, it will not only make longer trips possible for trains equipped with my invention but will also mark the time when what you see in front of you can be put into use in a practical way all over the world."

The train was approaching the largest incline. In front of it was the final pack of ore beneath the tracks. Although it had slowed down a bit, the train was going somewhat faster than it had been the last time it crossed one of those spots. Rolling over the next one caused its lights to flare even brighter and the train to shoot to a speed that was faster than it had acquired before.

After a few seconds of intense glowing, the lights along the side of the cars popped one by one.

The sparks pouring from the sides of the cars and engine blazed into a fire that singed grass on either side of the tracks.

Rattling as it climbed the steep incline, the engine tore down that section of track without slowing in the slightest. It was going so fast that, at the top of the incline, it snapped free from the tracks and sailed through the air for no less than twenty feet.

Clint instinctively grabbed Bertolucci by the collar to pull him away from the tracks, even though neither one of them were in any danger of being hit by the flying train. It was a good thing he kept his hold, however, since Bertolucci wanted to run to his creation before it even landed.

The train hit the ground with a jarring crash, portions of it catching on fire upon impact. The instant Clint let go of him, Bertolucci ran to the pile of smoking metal and wood. Clint went there as well, keeping his eyes and ears open for any hint that a larger explosion might be on its way.

Clint couldn't make out everything Bertolucci was saying as he rushed over to the wreckage of his experiment, but it was filled with a lot of, "Oh, what's wrong" and "My poor baby" sort of sentiments.

The first thing Clint noticed when he got close enough was the brackets along the bottom of the cars that were supposed to keep the train on the tracks had been melted and snapped into pieces.

Bertolucci touched one broken bracket, burning his finger on metal that had been heated by the overflow of sparks. "Needless to say, this . . . ummm . . . still requires some work."

Chapter Forty-Two

At first, Clint had felt more than a little embarrassed by the fact that Bertolucci had managed to build his little railroad behind the laboratory without being noticed. Of course, Clint had seen the doctor out there plenty of times but hadn't watched closely enough to know exactly what was going on. To his credit, where the doctor's work was concerned, Clint didn't hold out much hope of ever knowing everything that was going on.

Once he made a point to watch the doctor as closely as he tried to watch everything else, Clint realized there was no shame in losing track of Bertolucci's progress. Once the doctor got some momentum, he darted around his lab like a bee that couldn't decide which flower to harvest. He went in and out, built part of one thing before scribbling notes at his desk, all without pausing long enough to take a breath.

Giving up hope of making sense of it all, Clint waited until he could catch up with someone who wasn't too possessed by their purpose.

"Antonia!" he shouted to the young woman leaving the lab at the moment.

She picked her head up, gave him a tired smile and walked over to where Clint was standing. "Hello, Clint. What do you need?"

"How much longer does the doctor need?"

"For what?"

"To be finished," Clint said. "With all of this."

"All of this?" she asked with a weary laugh. "I don't think you understand how scientists work. He likely won't ever be finished with all of this."

"I mean with this project that's keeping him on this island. How much longer?"

"There are some railroad men coming by tomorrow. The doctor and I have been trying to get things ready for that."

"Tomorrow?"

She nodded.

"Why didn't I know about this?" Clint asked.

"I only just found out about it. Those railroad men have wanted to come here for some time, but Carmine keeps putting them off. This was probably going to be another one of those times, but something changed."

"What's changed?"

"He's made some sort of attachment to his engine," Antonia replied. "He says it will help to store up some of the extra energy provided by the ore. I've been trying to tell him for months that he needed to do that, but he insisted on going ahead and building his bigger model anyway." She glanced in the direction of the lab and dropped her voice to a whisper when she added, "I think he was trying to impress you."

"Impress me?"

"Yes."

"Why?"

"Come on, Clint. You must know why."

"I'm sure that I don't."

"You've already saved his life more than once," she told him. "When we're in a room together and you're somewhere else, it's all he can talk about."

"I doubt that very much," Clint scoffed. "He must talk about nothing other than his ore and machines."

"Well, I suppose he does. But you're the subject that comes in second and for him, that's saying quite a lot."

"Well, I'll take the compliment."

"Why were you asking about being through with this?" she asked. "Are you in a hurry to leave?"

"Not really. I'm just waiting for the other shoe to drop where those men are concerned. I've met too many like Holland and McPike to think for one moment that they'd just up and leave without coming back."

"That's exactly what Carmine thinks has happened. He's convinced they're too frightened of you to try anything else."

"If that is the case, then that's great. If not, those men will be coming back. If they do, I want to know the two of you can be safe. Is there any place around here you can hole up?"

"Hole what?"

"Hide out," Clint said. "You know, some room with a sturdy door you can lock or maybe even a cellar."

"There's a cellar beneath the lab and one beneath the house. Both are used for storage."

"Do they have doors that lock?"

"Yes." Wrapping her arms around herself as though a cold breeze had just blown in, Antonia asked, "What's wrong? Why are you worried about this now?"

"Because," Clint said, "they'll be coming."

Some of the color drained from Antonia's face. "Clint, you're scaring me."

"Good."

"Why is that good?"

"Because people make the worst mistakes because they're not afraid when they should be."

"Are you scared?"

"I'm concerned," he replied. "There's a difference. I suppose that's where fear starts, though. I've just had more practice at this sort of thing."

"What sort of thing?" Antonia's eyes drifted toward the Colt hanging at his side. "Oh. I see."

Chapter Forty-Three

Later that night, after the sun had set and the wind had died down to barely a whisper, they came. Clint could hear water slapping against the sides of the boat even before he could hear the chugging of its engine. He was sitting at one of the posts he'd chosen for its view of most of the shoreline when the sound caught his attention.

He ran for Eclipse's saddlebags, found the field glasses and put them to his eyes. Holland and Wesley were at the front of the boat, glaring into the darkness ahead of them as though they knew they were being watched. There were more men onboard. Clint could see movement, but not enough to get an accurate count. Something in his gut assured him they were there, however, and that was always enough for him.

After stuffing the glasses back into his bag, Clint climbed into his saddle and flicked the reins. Eclipse bolted into the shadows, having memorized every inch of the island they'd patrolled so much even before Clint had committed it to memory. A few minutes later, they were all in the same spots they'd been for their first meeting. Clint stood looking into the eyes of Wesley and Holland with the boat anchored behind them.

"Did you get the journals?" Holland asked.

"No," Clint said.

"What about any of the ore? Something useful from Berto-lucci's machines? A few pages of notes?"

"No to all three."

Holland's mouth formed a thin, tight line. The expression on his face showed disappointment mixed with some anger but not a bit of surprise.

"That's a shame," he said.

"Since this didn't turn out too well for you," Clint said, "perhaps you should just get in your boat and leave."

"We didn't come this far just to leave."

"Actually, you didn't really come very far at all," Clint said. "Texas is just a short boat ride in that direction. You could be back before you know it."

"I don't think you understand me," Holland said. "Either that, or you're being a smart-ass. Either way, I don't like it."

"You want honest? You want earnest? Fine. Get back in your boat and leave or I'll put you in it and set you adrift. I'll give you a kick toward the rest of Texas, but I won't guarantee where you'll land. You try anything other than that and . . ."

"And what?" Wesley snapped.

"Don't test me," Clint said evenly. "Just take my bit of free advice and be on your way."

Wesley smirked, but there was something about the way he smiled that made Clint uncomfortable. It was the confident grin of someone who'd already won the fight they were in and regarded whoever stood in front of him as nothing more than a minor obstacle to be stepped over at any given time.

Holland motioned to Wesley to hold off.

"Mister Adams," he said, "you've been given more time than I originally wanted to give you. I've dealt with Doctor

Bertolucci enough to know how stubborn he can be and how closely he guards his secrets."

Those words told Clint that Holland either didn't know Bertolucci very well or that the doctor truly trusted Clint enough to talk at length about nearly every little thing he'd been working on.

"You've had more than enough time to make your move," Holland continued. "And I'm being generous enough to give you one last chance. Get me the doctor's notes or the ore."

"Why not just take them yourself?" Clint challenged.

"Because I've already tried that and it didn't turn out well. If I need to go that way again, I will. Having someone close to him on my side would be much easier as well as profitable for all parties involved. Trust me, the more profit there is, the richer we all become."

After making a show of thinking for a few seconds, Clint said, "Go to hell."

Holland shrugged and motioned to Wesley one more time.

Wesley's confident smirk took on a murderous glint. A fraction of a second later, he drew his pistol and brought it up to fire.

Clint knew Wesley's intentions the moment he saw that glint in the other man's eye. By the time Wesley reached for his pistol, Clint had already cleared leather. As Wesley's pistol was about to fire, Clint's had already sent a round through the air to drill a hole through Wesley's chest.

All of the smug confidence evaporated from Wesley's face. His hand went limp and the pistol fell from it. Just to be sure, Clint knocked him down with another shot through the heart.

Wesley hit the ground hard on his back. His last breath exploded from his lungs, leaving him an empty, bloody mess.

Holland merely shook his head. "It's a shame, Adams. This could have happened so much easier."

"It's finished, Holland."

"You can't possibly believe that," Holland said as he backed toward the boat.

Clint was going to tell him to stop. He was about to command Holland to stay where he was so he could be brought in, but that was before Clint heard the gunshots coming from Bertolucci's compound.

Suddenly it was so clear. While Holland and Wesley had landed and had their deadly conversation with Clint, someone else had gotten onto the island to go straight for Bertolucci and Antonia.

"You've got a choice to make, Adams," Holland taunted and he kept heading toward the boat. "Come after me or see what you can do for the doctor. You're no cold-blooded killer, so I doubt you'll just—"

A shot from Clint's Colt shut Holland up real quickly.

Chapter Forty-Four

Clint merely had to jump in his saddle and snap the reins to launch Eclipse into a full gallop. Both of them knew the terrain so well by this point that they made it to one of Clint's higher scouting points without disturbing more than a few low-hanging branches along the way.

Once he was atop the tall hill, Clint pulled the rifle from his saddle's boot and sighted along the top of its barrel. There were a few targets to choose from. Two men stood outside the doctor's laboratory, firing in through the windows and another was beating on the front door of the house.

Guessing that Antonia was in the house, Clint fired on that man first. The rifle bucked against his shoulder, sending its round into the man knocking on the door. The impact spun the man to one side and caused him to bump against the door. His gun was already drawn so the man started firing in the general direction from which he'd been shot.

Clint calmly levered in another round, took a few seconds to aim and let out a slow breath. When the breath was complete, he squeezed his trigger. The bullet he fired caught the gunman in the center of his body, knocking him into the front of the house like a kick from a mule.

The house's front door opened and Antonia stuck her head outside. She looked around, but didn't see anything before the men outside the laboratory caught sight of her. Even though she was quick to pull herself inside and shut the door again, the damage had already been done. The other two gunmen saw what had happened to their partner and intended on repaying the death by spilling some blood themselves.

A few rounds were fired at Clint, none of which came anywhere close to hitting him. The next salvo was aimed at the one target they could see, which was the house where Antonia was hiding. Cursing under his breath, Clint took aim as best he could. He fired a few times in the direction of the gunmen before, even though he didn't have a clear bead. He was just trying to keep one of them from getting lucky with a shot through the house's window. Even more importantly, he wanted to discourage them from kicking down the door and going after Antonia with renewed vigor.

Clint knew he hit one of the gunmen, even if it was just a minor wound and not enough to put that man down. Those two weren't complete idiots, however, and quickly found some cover behind support posts and trees. Since he still didn't have a clear shot, Clint stuck the rifle back into its boot and tapped his heels against Eclipse's sides. The Darley Arabian tore down the hill, carrying Clint into the compound.

Even though he arrived in a matter of seconds, Clint couldn't help but feel he was already too late.

Gunfire erupted from the compound as one man standing in the open took shots at him. In the short amount of time that Clint took to get there, the gunmen had moved out of their hiding places and renewed their attack on the laboratory. One of them had even managed to bust open a window and was climbing inside.

Leaning down low against Eclipse's back, Clint rode as close as he dared before pushing away from the Darley Arabian and throwing himself from the saddle. Performing a move they'd practiced more than a few times over the years, Clint rolled in one direction while the Darley Arabian veered off in the other. The moment Clint came to a stop, he fired a trio of shots from his Colt.

The gunman who'd been caught in the open jerked and twitched as hot lead tore through him. His muscles quickly gave out and he crumbled into a heap. Clint walked forward, reloading his pistol and keeping his eyes on the lab.

"Antonia!" Clint shouted. "You all right?"

After a few gut-wrenching seconds, she shouted from the house, "I'm not hurt. Is it safe to come out?"

"Not yet. Stay put until I come for you."

Clint was at the lab's door by now. He kicked it open and stepped to one side, fully expecting the gunshots that ripped through the doorway and frame. One of those bullets came close enough to him that Clint could hear it tearing through the air in front of his face, but he didn't let that stop him from taking a quick look inside.

At the far end of the lab, Bertolucci was being held by the gunman who'd forced his way inside. The doctor was staggering and had a bloody face, but still tried to put up what little fight he could.

"What about you, doc?" Clint asked while walking in through the battered door frame. "Doing ok?"

"I've been better," the doctor replied after spitting out some blood. "But I'll pull through."

190

Thanks to the mostly open layout of the laboratory, Clint could see just about all there was to see from his position. The gunman and Bertolucci were near the doctor's desk which had been overturned in the scuffle. The back wall of the lab had been busted open to form a wide gap next to the machine that powered Bertolucci's equipment.

McPike was back there, his arms full of ledgers and papers. Dropping those, he pulled his gun from its holster. "Last Chance, Adams."

"To join you?" Clint shouted. "After all of this?"

"There's heaps of money to be made with this stuff! If the army of this country don't wanna buy this explosive ore, some other country will. Then there's the notes and whatever other shit is in these books that are worth more than gold to most of the same people plus a few others like this doctor here that're doin' research of their own!"

"You'd sell weapons to foreign countries?" Clint asked while taking a few steps forward. The man holding Bertolucci tensed, but kept glancing back at McPike for the order to do more than that.

"Armies are gonna shoot at each other no matter what," McPike said. "I served in one long enough to know that. Besides, this ain't the sort of thing that could burn a country down. There's plenty here to make a man rich, though. Mister Holland already proved that well enough."

"Holland's down," Clint said. "He'll either bleed out or will go to jail. Either way, he's no use to you."

McPike shrugged. "Don't matter none. I know who to sell this to. You wanna help, there's fewer ways to split the take."

"Not gonna happen," Clint said. He'd watched the man holding Bertolucci for long enough to decipher a pattern. When that gunman twitched back to look at McPike for a split-second, Clint fired a shot that clipped that man's elbow.

The gunman jerked to one side, his grip loosened enough for Bertolucci to wriggle free. As soon as he had a clear shot, Clint put a bullet through the gunman's chest and another through his head.

"Eh, to hell with all of you!" McPike snarled as he scooped up as much of the papers and ledgers as he could before bolting out of the lab.

Chapter Forty-Five

The back wall of the lab had been busted out with several planks cracked apart or simply pried loose and tossed aside. Clint approached the opening carefully, even though it was plain to see that nobody stood near it. Once outside, he could see the stream that powered the machine's paddlewheel. To his left was the open lot where Bertolucci's model train tracks had been laid down.

The stream was just large enough to power the wheel and just wide enough for a small boat to float from the back of the lab all the way into the gulf. Apparently, while Holland and his men had provided a distraction, that was exactly what McPike and his partners had done. Now, McPike was back on his boat and starting the small engine that would move it down the stream.

Before Clint could take another step, he felt a hand on his shoulder. "Wait a moment," Bertolucci said.

"I can't wait," Clint replied hastily. "If I get to my horse now I can catch that boat before it makes it into open water."

"Let it get out there."

"What? No! I won't have gone through this much only to let the son of a bitch get away."

"My work isn't worth it," Bertolucci said. "I want to be rid of it."

"You may be rid of it," Clint told him, "but whoever McPike sells it to will do plenty of damage on their own. You want that on your conscience?"

"No. I don't. That's why I made this." Bertolucci held out a closed fist and opened it to show what he'd been holding. They were three bullets. While the casings weren't anything special, the bullets themselves were a shiny metallic color that glinted in the light.

"Are these what I think they are?" Clint asked.

Bertolucci nodded solemnly. "I made them during one of my late night sessions. I took the liberty of examining your rifle and repurposing a few of the rounds. I hope you don't mind."

The boat was moving down the stream, but not fast enough for Clint to worry about it getting out of range before he could get to the rifle he kept in Eclipse's saddle. When he returned, McPike's boat was just starting to gain some speed.

Clint loaded his rifle with a few normal rounds as well as the ones Bertolucci had made and took careful aim.

"You sure about this?" he asked.

Bertolucci stood nearby. He nursed one of the welts on his face and winced. "Yes."

That was all Clint needed to hear. He wasn't familiar with everything that was in McPike's boat, but the narrow crates that had been stacked on its deck were easy enough to spot. Clint let out a breath and squeezed his trigger. The rifle sent its round through the air, knocking away some of the uppermost crate on the stack.

Clint's second round hit in the same spot, busting open one of the crates even wider. His next three rounds were Bertolucci's and he put every one of them into the crate that he'd already cracked open like an egg.

McPike shouted and fired back at the shore, but only managed to dig a few holes in the ground well short of where Clint was standing. There were no other shots being fired and no other men that Clint needed to worry about.

After a few more seconds, the crate that had been hit exploded with a muffled thump to send bits of wood and chunks of the boat's cabin and rails into the water. The boat continued to chug along, however, carrying McPike and his remaining cargo further away.

"I thought there'd be more," Clint said.

"Give it a few more seconds."

A few seconds later, the other crates exploded. Like rolling thunder, the muffled explosions ripped pieces out of the boat and sent them in opposite directions. McPike was just starting to jump overboard when the entire boat was engulfed in a massive blast. The shockwave from that explosion slammed into Clint and Bertolucci, knocking them down while shaking leaves on the branches around them.

"Is that all of the ore?" Clint asked as splinters and embers drifted down from above.

"Apart from a few samples that are still in my model's tracks, yes. I'll be destroying those as well."

"You could just pack them up and move your work somewhere else," Clint offered. "Somewhere you could start over with some privacy."

"I will start over, but not with this project. I've got other ideas. Ideas that aren't so destructive."

Clint stood up and dusted himself off. "Seems like a shame to waste so much time and effort."

"Science is a series of setbacks," Bertolucci said, accepting Clint's help to get to his feet. "We learn from mistakes and move on to the next, hopefully better, experiment. Do you think McPike is . . .?"

Nodding as he watched a few pieces of the gunman sink in the stream, he nodded and said, "Yeah. He sure is."

"What about Holland?"

"I'll get him and take him back to Galveston. He's done more than enough here to wind up in a jail cell. Also, I'm betting there are some railroad men who'd like a word with him."

"Some of those are rough types," Bertolucci said.

"Yep." Looking down at his rifle, Clint asked, "What did you make those bullets out of, anyway?"

"The same element that was found in Holland's hammer. I kept some as a way to dispose of my scrap ore. The explosion is actually quite clean. There were also some new additions I made to the silver coating."

Clint started walking through the lab toward the house so he could let Antonia know it was safe for her to come out. Along the way, Bertolucci explained every little detail surrounding the bullets he'd made and the reaction that had blown up the boat along with McPike. Clint barely understood a word of it.

Coming Soon!

THE GUNSMITH
432
The Bank Job

Visit us at www.speakingvolumes.us

Now Available

THE GUNSMITH
430
Show Girl

Visit us at www.speakingvolumes.us

Coming Spring 2018

Lady Gunsmith 5
The Portrait of Gavin Doyle

For more information
visit: www.speakingvolumes.us

Now Available

ANGEL EYES *series*
by
Award-Winning Author
Robert J. Randisi (J.R. Roberts)

Visit us at www.speakingvolumes.us

Now Available

TRACKER *series*
by
Award-Winning Author
Robert J. Randisi (J.R. Roberts)

Now Available

MOUNTAIN JACK PIKE *series*
by
Award-Winning Author
Robert J. Randisi (J.R. Roberts)